Stories That Need to Be Told 2025

STORIES
THAT NEED
TO BE TOLD
2025

Edited by

Jennifer Top

TULIPTREE
PUBLISHING, LLC

The answer is always Love.
Or Bob Dylan.

Contents

Contents

Tummy

Matt Landig

I'd always prided myself on never getting my heart broken.
Somehow I'd attained the seemingly unattainable, the New York unicorn for single college girls: a stable boyfriend. My girlfriends always said to me, "Claudia, you're so lucky," as they told me their boyfriend frustrations and then, weeks later, of their breakups. Invariably I'd listen to the former and console them during the latter, but I never could extinguish a slight tingle of superiority. I knew Noelle should never have hooked up with that brooding (read: narcissistic) bass player, that Simone should never have started anything with that professional gamer (read: loser), and that Alicia should never have given that fun-loving (read: perpetually drunk) intern the time of day. The worst part was that it had been the guys doing the dirty deed of dumping, leaving my girlfriends in tears. I consoled myself with the knowledge that—conceited as it may sound—I would never make such misguided decisions, that I had a great boyfriend, that I always made sensible relationship decisions, and that, at 22, I had everything under control.

Until my boyfriend Douglas dumped me.

It was remarkably simple how it happened. We had just said goodbye to our friend Mitch and sat down at our usual corner table at P.J. Clarke's. I plowed through my usual burger, my beloved P.J. Clarke's burger—deliriously moist and juicy, the buns cradling the lettuce, tomatoes, onions, pickles, mayo, and meat—and its perfect counterpart, the truffle fries, lavishly dusted with parmesan. I usually didn't eat like this, but when P.J. Clarke calls, one must follow. It also helped that I had the metabolism of two teenage boys.

"Damn, these are always so good," I said, dipping three thin fries into a tiny cup of sauce. "I think I may love garlic aioli *almost* as much as I love you."

Normally, a comment like this was the cue for Douglas to lunge for my fries, scooping them up in big fists, while I'd give them tiny, quick slaps. "Get your own!" I'd say in mock outrage. But now—none of that. In fact, he winced when I made my aioli joke. I frowned. Something was up.

Douglas sat, unusually taciturn and, in fact, ridiculously businesslike, his hands folded on the table, his eyes downcast. "I have something to tell you. I don't know how to say it."

"What is it?" I asked. A vague tightness took hold of my stomach. I felt a bomb about to detonate.

Douglas tried looking at me; he couldn't. I could see his cheeks growing hot and red. "I've been seeing—uh, sleeping with—uh, seeing someone else," he said.

I couldn't feel my stomach. I couldn't feel anything.

"Who is it?" I don't remember if I looked at him when I asked. I couldn't believe that I could still form a sentence. "Is it someone I know?"

He nodded.

In my mind I flipped through all the names of our mutual friends, my best friends. "Is it Simone? Noelle? Alicia?"

He paused. "It's Mitch."

A soft, mute explosion. Everything turned white.

Mitch was a fellow classmate in the NYU music program. Since the beginning of freshman year, the three of us had been as inseparable as musketeers, if you can imagine musketeers lunching in the student dining hall, philosophizing in dark-paneled pubs in Tribeca, and dancing in after-hours clubs—*straight* clubs. When had Douglas and Mitch turned gay? Why hadn't I realized it? Do people even *turn* gay—like autumn leaves changing color in Central Park? And wait a minute: Who seduced whom?

I can't get into this, I told myself. I won't feel this. I won't feel.

Douglas crumbled; he babbled, he apologized, he said he still wanted us to be friends. I stared at the red checkered tablecloth and wondered why he'd chosen this place to murder me. When he started to cry, my gaze shifted to my left boot. I have no feeling, I thought. No emotion. I mumbled noncommittal nonsense and pushed my chair back, flinching at the scraping noise. As I got up to leave, I glanced down at the remains of my food and shuddered—a disgusting heap of crap. I thought, I'm never eating a burger and fries. Ever again.

I thought I'd be able to deal with the breakup. But the sensible old me was cracked, broken. "Of course you feel broken," Alicia said as she slid her arms around me in an embrace I knew I didn't deserve. "That's why they call it a *break*-up." Noelle and Simone took their turns to comfort me too, but all I could think of was how patronizing, how arrogant, how smug I must have been when they'd come to *me* for comfort. (Or had they noticed?) I couldn't get over the fact that I couldn't get over Douglas. Concentrating on anything important was futile, and what was worse: I couldn't use Manhattan as a distraction. My favorite bagel place, Bagel Bob's, was *verboten*; Douglas and I would go there almost every Saturday after music rehearsals. Standing in line for Broadway tickets reminded me of the times when I'd stand in line with Douglas. Going to a concert at Alice Tully Hall at Lincoln

Center? Forget it—that's where Douglas and I first held hands, three years ago. And P.J. Clarke's—my heavenly, wonderful P.J. Clarke's—was obviously out of the question.

Douglas and I (and Mitch) lived in the same residence halls; I couldn't begin to deal with seeing Douglas (or Mitch), so I'd have to find another place to live (thanks, Mitch). I realized I should steer clear of the entire Village, but where did that leave me? I didn't like Brooklyn and hated Queens. I thought, I got it, the Upper West Side! But no, that was Douglas's and my favorite neighborhood. We'd wander the narrow streets of warm, brick brownstones, pointing at ones we liked. (We'd thought about moving in together, after graduation.) At Central Park we'd meet up with Mitch (yuck), and we'd all throw stones in the reservoir and crack jokes. (Oh my God, wait a minute—sometimes as a comedy routine they'd pretend to be a gay couple. They'd actually affect lisps, hold hands, and pretend to kiss. In front of me. What the hell were they thinking? What the hell had I thought?)

I wandered around the city staring at apartments, lofts, co-ops—it was all pointless; I was going to run into Douglas anyway, or worse, run into *them*, holding hands—for real. Laughing. I hated them. And then I immediately felt guilty: I'm not supposed to hate gay people, but I can't help it, he went behind my back, he betrayed me, and now I'll never find another boyfriend, Douglas was the only boy who thought I was pretty, we had so many good times together, and how could he do this, I don't even recognize him anymore, and what does that even *mean*, and where am I going to live, oh wait, what about here, this place looks cool, but it's a block from the H&M, the one Douglas and I always shop at, and I hate H&M anyway, their clothes make me look like a boy, I look like a boy, a freakishly tall, flat-chested boy with hopeless hair, I look like a boy, but *hey! that's probably why Douglas liked me!* but he *doesn't* like me, that point has now been made abundantly, *fuckingly* clear, and I hate him, I hate him, I hate him, stop hating him, he can't help being who he is, why can't you accept him, but why can't he accept *me*, why can't he like *me*, why can't I look beautiful like Noelle, have fantastic boobs like Simone, be gorgeously curvy like Alicia, oh God, am I a lesbian, it would serve me right to be the only homophobic lesbian in the world, oh God, here's Bagel Bob's, fuck you, Bagel Bob, screw you, P.J. Clarke's, and fuck you Alice Tully, I bet your husband loved you and you were beautiful and your figure was a fucking *hourglass* and your husband built Lincoln Center for you because you were beautiful and no one is ever going to love me enough to build *anything* for *me*, and no one is ever going to love me the way Douglas probably loves Mitch so fuck you Mitch and most of all fuck fuck *fuck* you Douglas and I hate men and I hate women and I'm just going to be asexual and move to Connecticut.

I stopped walking, winded. I wanted to gather breath, enough breath to scream and yell and howl into the air, up into the buildings, but there were people everywhere. And yet I was alone. I hated New York, and I didn't exist.

I had to call Grandma.

As the subway hurtled toward Grandma's apartment in Murray Hill, I vowed not to think about Douglas. I wasn't going to think about Douglas. I refused to think about Douglas.

This wasn't working.

Give yourself a topic.

My cello concerto. I have to practice my Elgar cello concerto for Monday. Oh God, I haven't picked up my bow in two days. Douglas and Mitch are probably practicing right now, and—

No, Claudia. Try again.

Okay: Zabar's. I thought about the raspberry linzer tortes at Zabar's. I want a dozen raspberry linzer tortes from Zabar's. But I couldn't of course: I didn't really have breasts or a figure, but I didn't want a stomach, either. I couldn't wreck my life by eating everything in sight, ballooning. Noelle, an art history major, had once showed me a picture of the Venus of Willendorf, the oldest found art object—a dinky, mottled figure, but with giant breasts drooping onto her massive tummy. Many art historians thought the Venus of Willendorf was intended as the quintessential female or a fertility symbol, but Noelle's interpretation was strictly modern-day cautionary: "This is what I'm gonna look like if I keep eating lasagna. You don't know how lucky you are, Claude—you're not fat and you're not too thin. I hate you." She laughed.

I thought about Douglas's body, buff, even slightly stocky, the confident way he moved it. I thought about his body, naked and thick, folding over Mitch's small, slender one and wondered if that was the problem that started everything: that Douglas couldn't fold his body over mine, that I was too tall, not needy enough, too sensible to ever have wants that he could fulfill, problems that he could solve. Oh God, I felt so stupid. What had I been doing in the relationship? I couldn't give him anything; I had been a big fucking fraud. No, stop: *He* was the fraud. Were all our intimate moments a lie? Why hadn't I realized that he was gay? Did I just completely turn him off women? No, that's ridiculous—isn't it?

My head started burning; I massaged my temples, a pointless exercise. Was I ready for another relationship? What kind of person do I need to be? How in the world would I ever get to be a girlfriend, a wife? Or—oh my God—a mother?

The subway lurched to my stop. As I climbed the steps, up into the uncharacteristically silent darkness of the city, its streets surprisingly depleted of people, I found myself staring at a café window. Underneath a huge glass cloche, nestled like newborns, lay two chubby bagels.

Then I did something I hadn't done in forever. I began to cry.

Thank God the elevator in Grandma's building was empty; I had time to redo my mascara. Staring into my compact, I thought, Oh God, I look like a cross between a panda and Marilyn Manson. I wiped the sludge away. Douglas did this to you, I thought. Don't let him off the hook.

Grandma lived in a beautiful high-rise with magnificent views of uptown and of the East River. New Yorkers had given Murray Hill the dubious distinction of being the only boring neighborhood of Manhattan. But tell that to Grandma, and she'd say, "Nonsense! All of New York is fascinating. And if you don't think so, well then, you're not looking hard enough."

After Grandpa's death last year, Grandma kept her spirit. My parents kept suggesting that she move closer to them, upstate, but staying in the city felt right to her; at 76, she was still self-sufficient and still had more energy than most of my friends. And her staying in the city gave me the chance to spend more time with her.

I'd never liked calling my grandmother "Grandma." Everybody does it, but it seemed cornpone, especially for a woman who had started her life in ballet and then as an actress on Broadway. On the other hand, "Grandmother" seemed stiff and too formal for her personality, and she balked at my calling her "Claire" or even the compromise moniker "Grandma Claire." Grandma had friends who insisted their grandchildren refer to them by their first names, but she herself scorned this practice. "They're just afraid of age," she said to me once. "The word 'grandma' reminds them that they're not young anymore. But 'Grandma' is what I am to you, my dear. And I will never stop being your grandma."

I knocked on her door, hoping she wouldn't notice any trace of tears. I hadn't told her much over the phone—just asked if I could see her, it's been too long, just wanted to see how you were, I'm fine, I'm totally fine, I'm great—

"How did it happen?" Grandma opened the door. Even in my state, I noticed she looked sensational—a pale violet sweater set and a scarf splashed with irises. But wait: How did she know about the breakup? She looked at me, stricken. "Oh, sweetheart—I knew something was wrong. All that talk and not a word about Douglas."

I burst into tears again. I immediately wanted to kick myself in the face: *twice* in one day. I must be going for some sort of record: World's Biggest Crybaby. But Grandma calmly, wordlessly took my hand in hers, led me into the living room, and sat me down.

I told her everything, in dizzyingly nonsensical non-order. Then I told her everything again. I babbled, I bitched, I moaned. Eventually, my words and my tears dried up; I settled into dazed silence, a trauma coma.

Grandma, usually in constant motion, always ready with a perfectly timed joke that would keep her dancer and actor friends roaring at parties, sat silently through my tirade, offering me the occasional Kleenex. She seemed contemplative, serene as Confucius.

"What should I do, Grandma?"

She paused for a long time. Then she said, "My dear—my experience with matters of the heart is this: All advice is useless. Your heart simply isn't ready for any of it. But that doesn't mean all is hopeless, or that there is nothing you *can* do. On the contrary, you must do two very important things if you are going to get through this. The first thing—and you're already doing it and quite well—is that you must cry."

My fingers involuntarily wiped off runny mascara that I couldn't see.

"And the second thing is that," she paused dramatically, "you must eat ice cream."

Was she serious?

"I don't get it. You're joking, right?"

"Come with me." She took my hand into hers, pulled me up from the sofa, and guided me to the kitchen. We stopped in front of the stainless-steel refrigerator.

With a flourish, she flung open the freezer door. A burst of cold flew through the air. Six frozen cartons of ice cream sat perched on the top shelf amid snowy crystals. Grandma smiled, gesturing with a ringmaster's sweep of her hand.

"Meet my two boyfriends: Ben and Jerry! If you play your cards right," her eyes twinkled, "I'll share them with you."

She set the ice cream on the counter. One carton showed a cartoon cow holding a giant cherry, playing it like a ukulele; on another, a cow in a chef's hat held a wooden spoon— looking as bewildered as I was. Why did Grandma have *this* much ice cream? It couldn't have been for me; Manhattan's culinary offerings had turned me into a gelato girl.

She said, "Cherry Garcia and Chocolate Fudge Brownie. Which one are you having?" She looked at me with the sudden, hushed solemnity of a game show host expecting the correct answer to the million-dollar question.

Hell, I didn't know. Which one had fewer calories? I held up a tentative finger in the direction of Cherry Garcia.

"Wrong. You will have both." Grandma opened the lids and produced a stainless-steel ice cream scooper from a nearby drawer.

"But, Grandma, I don't—I don't understand what you're trying to—"

"My dear—you've just had your heart broken. Although it doesn't seem this way now, you will feel better. But this is how you are going to heal: You will continue to cry," she paused, "and you will eat ice cream."

I didn't know how to react. I landed on a random thought: "But won't I get cellulite?"

"Cellulite? Let's call it what it is, dear—it's fat. Plain and simple. But to answer your question: yes," she said, looking at me. "You might get fat. If you do, you will lose the fat. But maybe not entirely. There might be a *little* bit of fat that will linger." She chuckled. "That's the price of heartbreak. Why do you think I have this?" With a conspiratorial smile, she gestured to her stomach.

I'd never noticed before—probably because of Grandma's posture or charm or beauty or energy—the faintest suggestion of a tummy pressing against her pale purple sweater. And then I realized why Grandma had all that ice cream: Grandpa. She was going through her own heartbreak.

"Now don't get me wrong. I'm not crazy about having this tummy. Most people would hate having something like this. I know people who've had liposuction. Tummy tucks. Even had their stomachs stapled. But your old grandma has come to realize a few things over the years. And one thing I've learned is that this tummy is my badge of honor. It tells me that I have loved. And that I have *been* loved. And once you, my dear, are done with the process of crying and eating ice cream, once you are done with that whole rigmarole, you will come to realize that you, too, have loved. I'm proud of you for that. And though you may not believe it," she stroked my cheek with the front of her hand, "you have been loved, too."

She must have sensed that I was about to cry again, because she suddenly became crisply authoritative. "All right now, scoot! This looks like it's thawing out. Let your grandma fix you the best ice cream you've ever had!" She shooed me away with wild swoops of her hand, as if I were a giant stork that had flown through an open window.

Sniffling, I grabbed more Kleenex and trotted back to the living room. I peered at the New York skyline, silent, wiping underneath my eyes and blowing my nose. I didn't even want to look at my compact again, what with all the tears and snot and God-knows-what-else. And shit, this is the *third* time today, I thought, reaching for another Kleenex. And then I thought: Who cares? According to Grandma, I'm going to be doing a lot of crying, so I may as well get used to it.

I found my favorite armchair, sank into it, and let it hug me. After a while, I flopped my arms out on either side of me, then slowly draped them around my shoulders. I began to feel warm—and a little less disgusting. Yeah, okay. I feel okay.

I kicked off my shoes and padded to the kitchen doorway. "Grandma? Do you think I'm wrong to blame Douglas? I can't figure out if he's a good person or an—" I stopped just before the word "asshole," changing the word for Grandma's sake. "A jerk."

She appeared in the doorway. "Well," she said, sighing, "he was a fool to have let you down. And to have been dishonest with you. But Claudia, I don't think he meant to do you harm. I think this Mitch person exists for him in a way that you don't exist for him. And maybe in a way that no one else exists for him. He's following his heart."

He's following his *dick*, I thought, but I kept that to myself.

Grandma said, "Or it could be that he's just horny."

I stared at Grandma, my mouth open.

"What, Claudia? Why are you looking at me like that? After all, he's a man. And a gay man at that."

"Grandma! Aren't you being a little unfair? Aren't those stereotypes?"

She looked at me and laughed. "Hon. You don't get to be in the theater without knowing these things. I could tell you stories."

Grandma had dirt to dish? I looked at her expectantly.

"Another time, Claudia. Anyway, my guess is that Douglas is trying to figure himself out. And when you try to figure yourself out, sometimes you realize that you need something—or someone—other than what you have. So sometimes when you change, you end up hurting someone, even if it's unintentional. And I'm not proud of this, but I have to say," she paused, "that I'm no saint when it comes to the relationship department."

Something in her eyes told me she didn't want to go further. But now there was so much I wanted to know about her, so much that had been closed off to me. Maybe there were things she would never tell me. We let the silence between us grow. Why did people have such huge pieces of themselves hidden away? It wasn't fair.

"Come back to Earth, Claudia," Grandma crooned. "You're lost in thought, my dear. How are you holding up?"

I thought for a moment. "I feel so guilty. I keep blaming him. I know it's not his fault, but I keep thinking about how much of an—a jerk he was to me." Once again I'd almost said "asshole" but edited myself for Grandma's sake; I'd never heard her swear, at least not that I could remember.

"Well," Grandma said, "one of the few advantages of a breakup is that you get to decide what you want your ex to be. So let's make him a jerk. Later you may change your mind about that. But right now, because he broke your heart, let's make him," she paused, "an asshole." And with a wink, she popped back into the kitchen.

I burst out laughing—the first time today. I felt lighter, warmer, a little hopeful. Maybe I wouldn't have to do as much crying as Grandma predicted.

Resettling into the armchair, I gazed out the window at the Manhattan skyline, at all the windows, all the squares of light. I wondered how many buildings, how many homes, how many stores and shops I could see. And then I realized that all the buildings and institutions and shops existed without me: NYU and H&M and Alice Tully Hall, Bagel Bob's, and even P.J. Clarke's. They existed outside of me, unaware of my pain. If I hated New York, it didn't matter to New York; it would still go on without me, untouched by my feelings. And then I thought about how many people existed in each square of light.

But I existed, too. I existed without them, independent of them. Right now, I existed in a square of light, which others right now were looking at, longingly. Douglas didn't need me anymore, but I existed outside of him, too.

And then I felt a shift, something turning over and over inside me, something trying to emerge. I didn't know how I'd end up feeling about Douglas. I didn't know how I'd end up feeling about myself. But I knew I would understand what I needed to understand—in time.

"Nourishment." Grandma set a huge bowl onto my lap, then lifted my feet and slid an ottoman underneath. Then she settled in the armchair next to mine, propped up her feet on her ottoman, and began eating from her own bowl.

I looked down at my ice cream, a miniature planet: Cherry and vanilla tectonic plates sat propped against gigantic ice floes of chocolate fudge with brownie strata. To the side sat two little madeleines, the ends of their golden bodies lightly coated with carnival sprinkles.

I ate. Cherries and chocolate and cookies and fudge, vanilla and sprinkles and sugar and cream. I didn't need anything else. I didn't care about anything else—until I remembered something that in my selfishness I had forgotten to say. "I'm sorry about Grandpa."

She looked at me, smiled, took my hand in hers, and held it. We stayed that way for a while. Then she got up, releasing my hand with a playful shake, and took our bowls to the kitchen. She came back with more ice cream. I didn't protest; I simply took the bowl.

We sat in content silence, Grandma and I, slowly eating our ice cream, then slowly licking both sides of our spoons. We looked at each other and laughed. "Will you look at us?" Grandma cried. "All of New York out and about on a Saturday night and here *we* are, high up in our castle. They may think they know what's what, but *this*," she gestured around the apartment, "is how the beautiful people live!"

Yes, I thought, nodding, that was it. We were royalty, two beautiful women aloft on ottomans overlooking the night sky, the city glittering, winking to get our attention.

An idea pinpricked me, a minor idea, but I had to ask: "Grandma? Does any of this stuff have gluten in it?"

Grandma arched an eyebrow. "I certainly hope so," she said. "Now hush up and keep eating."

Sylvester: A Love Story
R.C. Goodwin

"Something I heard on the radio caught my attention when
I drove to work this morning," Yolanda said as we were
having dinner. "An interview with a psychologist named Joel
Kramer."

"Um hum?" Half-listening, I pushed a hillock of mashed
potatoes around the plate. At the time I had little appetite.

"He has a specialty, I guess you could call it, that's kind
of unusual. He sees patients who've had extreme or unusual
reactions to the death of pets. His wife's a veterinarian, which
is how he got interested in it. Sometimes she knew people
who grieved for months. For a year or more, even. A few of
them became suicidal." She paused to take a bite of meatloaf.
"I thought I'd pass it on to you."

"I'm not suicidal, not now, not ever." This was true, almost.

"Okay, you're not suicidal, but still . . ."

"But still, what?"

Her voice turned louder and tighter. "Half a year now.
It's been almost *half a year* since that cat died, and you barely
eat or sleep, and you don't smile, much less laugh, and our sex
life is close to nil. You're in perpetual mourning, you're not
right—"

Prickly and irascible, I interrupted her. "I go to work, I
play squash, I help Marisol with her homework." Marisol was
my 13-year-old stepdaughter, spending the week with her

father in the Dominican Republic. "I do half the cooking and vacuuming, I volunteer at Red Cross blood drives. I live my life, such as it is."

All this was true but misleading. At work I performed on autopilot, and I played squash barely concerned if I won or lost, and I couldn't have cared less about the blood drives. I had to force myself to concentrate on Marisol's math homework as if she were studying advanced calculus instead of beginning algebra.

"You're in perpetual mourning," Yolanda repeated. "You need to see that doctor. Or someone else, I don't care who. You need to do *something*." Her voice softened. "I don't want to live like this, Eli. I won't."

I take a certain perverse pride in having made it to the age of 42 without assistance from mental health helpers. I weathered the family's moves from New England to Louisiana to Oregon as my father climbed the academic ladder. He has a PhD; so far he has taught at six universities in four states. From kindergarten through high school I attended seven or eight different schools. I weathered my parents' fights, which could last for days or weeks, and my brother's autism—he might slug you if you touched him by accident as you crossed paths in the hallway. I weathered my sister's drinking. She missed my first wedding; she was going through detox for the third time or whatever. I weathered my divorce, and my current marriage has had its share of tailspins too. I've weathered the death of friends and family members, and, for better or worse, I've weathered all of it on my own. My parents agreed on this, if on few other things: *Keep your personal business to yourself.* Privacy is sacrosanct.

There's something else. Oliver Firkins, one of my college roommates, was a piece of work. Stoned half the time, he loved his shrooms as well. He was phobic about driving over bridges, dwarfs, and fireflies. Yes, fireflies. When his girlfriend dumped him (she was a married nonbinary exotic dancer 15 years his senior), he took to his bed for a week, like the heroine in a bloodless Victorian novel. The gist of it: Oliver was among the three or four strangest twits I've ever known, against stiff competition. He became a shrink.

Yolanda kept at it in the week ahead. Telling me, over and over, how extreme and frankly morbid my grieving had become. Telling me how it was ruining my life, and hers too. Initially sympathetic, she became by turns confused, bewildered, and incensed. The bombshell came one night in late June as we lay in bed, wide awake, our bodies not touching. When she spoke, her voice was devoid of anger but unyielding. "If you're still like this by Labor Day, I'm outta here." A statement of fact, not lending itself to argument.

"Eli Stern?" Dr. Kramer came into his waiting room, introduced himself, and offered his hand. Bald, thin to the point of ascetic, he had an inch or two and about five years on me. He guided me into his inner office, decorated mainly with pictures of dogs, cats, and the occasional parrot and pony.

I'd considered my opening gambit. The factual—*I'm a middle-level insurance drone who dislikes his job but doesn't know what else to do with his life. The pathology in my family could provide plots for several bad screenplays.* The vague but truthful—*I haven't been myself at all. I tolerate other people but have no interest in them, and I can't remember the last time I enjoyed something.* The most honest—*I don't want to be here but I'm afraid my wife will leave me if I don't see* someone.

None of which had anything to do with what I actually said. "I know you see people who've lost pets," I began.

"Sylvester died. My cat. Eight months ago, closer to nine. Jesus *Christ*, I loved that cat!" Then I began to cry, to sob, probably for no more than a minute or two but at the time it seemed like half an hour.

"This is ridiculous," I told him, wiping my eyes with the sleeve of my sweater. "He was just a cat, I know, I know. There are people with *real* problems. My cousin's son has leukemia, he's going through chemo at Dana Farber. One of my best friend's parents died on United 93. And it's not as though I'm living in some godforsaken corner of the Middle East or Africa—"

"Your problem looks real enough to me," the doctor broke in, handing me a box of Kleenex from his desk.

"Cats die on you, you're lucky if they last 15 years. It's just the way things are." I tried to sound calmer and more rational than I felt. "They die on you, and you get used to it."

"Apparently not." Kramer had interesting eyes, gray with a hint of green, the eyes of an empathetic man but one who brooked no nonsense. "Sylvester, his name was? What happened to him?"

I willed myself to stay coherent. "We were coming home one Saturday night from a movie. I saw him on the road, no more than 20 yards from our driveway. He had tuxedo markings, black with a white chest, like the cat in those Sylvester and Tweety Bird cartoons. Distinctive coloring. I knew right away it was him but kept hoping, *hoping*, I was wrong. He'd been hit by a car, it must have been only minutes earlier, he was still *warm*! I kneeled down and held him . . ."

I found it impossible to go on.

"Tell me more about him."

"I can't, not yet, I'd just start to . . . suppose I talk about cats in general. Why they're important to me."

"Go ahead."

"I grew up with cats. At one point we had four of them. My parents and my sister and I all liked them. Loved them. Even my useless violent brother did. We moved around, it seemed like we moved every year, and they made living in so many places tolerable. I know dogs are supposedly more attached to people and cats to places, but frankly I think that's a crock. Those cats were *there* for us; they were as attached to us as we were to them. You could count on them in a way you couldn't count on people. At least the people in our family."

"So it was safe to love them. Not only that, they loved you back, in their fashion."

I nodded. "We didn't do well at expressing love in our family. My father was a professor of geology . . . he did it by regaling us with theories of double subductions and trench migrations. My mother did it by plying us with rugelach and strudel, enough to make an elephant diabetic. Zeke, my autistic brother, if he loved us at all, expressed it by not hitting us for a while. My sister Franny did it by refraining from sarcasm, her weapon of choice, which got worse when she drank. Which she started to do at fifteen."

Dr. Kramer crossed his legs and jotted down notes on a legal pad. "Let's go back to cats. What else did you like about them?"

"Pretty much everything. Their grace, the way they move, as if they've all taken yoga lessons. Their aura of mystery. You never know what's on their mind, or exactly where you stand with them, or what they'll do next. There's a theory that the question mark was inspired by the curvature of a cat's tail." I took an odd comfort in the rambling. "Their famous independence, I like that too. I read somewhere that dictators hate cats. It figures. Try to imagine Hitler with a cat. He tells the cat, *Whenever I walk into the room, you will raise your right front paw and meow!* The cat stares at him disdainfully and says *go fuck yourself, Adolf!* Cats are a great example of what God can do when he's at his best, maybe to apologize for creating tobacco and mosquitos."

We veered away from cats, and he asked about me and my family. I felt relieved, since I still wasn't ready to talk about Sylvester. So I rambled again, about my father's stony silences and my mother's nonstop nervous patter. About growing up as the youngest of three, the designated normal one with a walled-off brother who dwelled miserably in his private universe, and a usually plastered sister. About religion, and my parents' ambiguity about it. We were twice-a-year Jews, Rosh Hashanah and Yom Kippur, who neither fully embraced Judaism nor broke with it. My first marriage, to a nice Jewish girl who did everything right, for which I could never forgive her. My two cardinal sins, parentally speaking: my second marriage, to a Greek-Latina divorcee with a six-year-old daughter who had cystic fibrosis, and my not becoming an MD.

The meeting flew by in a blur until Kramer said we were running out of time. We agreed to meet one week hence. On the way home it occurred to me that I'd made little mention of Sylvester, apart from the circumstances of his death. Nonetheless, something about the session had left me a bit unburdened.

Just before I left Kramer's office I turned to him. "I'm sorry," I said.

"What for?"

"For that unseemly emotional display. Believe it or not, that's the first time I cried since he was killed."

He briefly put his hand on my shoulder as I headed for the door. "You must have been way overdue."

I felt more composed when I saw him next, or at least less ragged. Ready or not, I'd resolved to take on the main order of business. "I want to talk about Sylvester," I opened.

Kramer nodded.

"He was our only cat together. Yolanda could take them or leave them, but eventually she agreed to one. Marisol, my stepdaughter, was my ally. She'd always wanted one, but her father was allergic to them. A coworker had a cat who'd had kittens and we went to her house. One of the kittens had that black and white color scheme I've always liked, probably from those cartoons I used to watch. He wouldn't stop looking at us. At me, in particular. None of the others paid attention to us, but *he* did. He walked over to us and began to rub his face against my hand. Now I'm sure this sounds crazy, but I swear it's as if he was waiting for me. I knew on the spot that *he's the one*. Marisol was also taken with him. In fact, she named him. She'd liked those cartoons too.

"Cats can take a while to settle in, but Sylvester made himself at home immediately. He went from room to room as he checked them all, giving each one his seal of approval. He liked all of us, but I was the clear favorite. He'd lay beside me, not them, just me. He'd lay as close as he could get. And there was this, he was the most playful cat I've ever known. He'd play with Yolanda and Marisol too, but eventually he'd get tired of it. With me he just kept on going. As a rule, I'm not what you'd call playful. I tend to be serious to the point of tiresome."

Kramer raised his eyebrows. "So, when you played with him, you felt freer than you usually were. That's important, don't you think?"

"I suppose." I must have sounded uncertain.

"I don't know about your being tiresome, but you do come across as pretty serious. It makes sense, given how you've described your family and your upbringing. Unlikely that you'd wind up frivolous."

"Frivolous. No, not exactly . . ."

"So Sylvester gave you permission to be more playful," continued Kramer. "Freer, as I said before. Freer, as I'm thinking you wanted to be, even though you may not have acknowledged it yourself."

Mulling this over, I stopped talking. He was the one to break the silence. "Tell me more about your playing. What kinds of things did you do with him?"

"Oh, nothing out of the ordinary. I'd give him a cloth mouse to chase around. Or I'd use a laser-like light, kind of a miniature flashlight. I'd point it on the wall or floor and he ran after it. Or I'd give him catnip, which he loved. He rolled around in it orgiastically." I rummaged through my memories of the two of us. Of massaging his face and chin while he half-closed his eyes, like a luxuriating potentate. Of gently pulling his tail. Of having fake fights with him—he'd bat away my hand, never with his claws out, and I'd bat away his paw. Of throwing him onto the bed, often from a distance of ten feet or so. The catapult, we called it.

"He was far and away the most *companionable* cat I've ever known," I said as our session was winding down. "I went for physical therapy when I hurt my back, and they gave me exercises to do at home. I did them every morning before I went to work. I'd lay on my back in the living room, and he sat next to my head. I told people facetiously that we used to be gay lovers in our previous lives. Maybe not so facetiously."

The world was becoming blurry. "God*dammi*t, I thought I could actually get through this session without crying."

"Why do you fight it so hard?"

Taking a Kleenex, I didn't answer him; I only shrugged.

"How often does this happen?" he asked a few moments later.

"The crying? It doesn't. Before that first time I met with you, it must have been half a decade ago. I haven't cried but I've been morose as hell. I try not to bring down Yolanda and Marisol, not that I've succeeded."

With that, Kramer changed direction. He began to toss questions at me like grapeshot. About my appetite and sleeping. About my level of energy (diminished), and my attention and concentration (ordinarily focused, I was newly scatterbrained), and my ability to enjoy things (for the most part, nonexistent). And then came the critical one: Was I suicidal?

"No, not exactly. But sometimes I'll go to bed and wish I'd die in my sleep."

Another pause. "I'd like to continue meeting with you, but I'd also like you to see a psychiatrist. I think you could benefit from medication."

"*No way!*" My volume and rancor startled both of us. Embarrassed, I recounted my experience with the supremely peculiar Oliver Firkins. Kramer smiled and even laughed at one point.

"I had in mind someone less exotic," he reassured me. "Besides, it's ridiculous to assume all psychiatrists are like that." He jotted down a name and number on a piece of paper and handed it to me. So it was that ten days later I met with Dr. Gloria Aaronson, an altogether normal-seeming woman of about 35 who struck me as unlikely to be paralyzed by a fear of dwarfs or fireflies. She asked me questions similar to Joel

Kramer's, wrote me a prescription for something called Viibryd, and made an appointment to see me in a month.

Kramer had a vacation coming up, so I didn't see him for three weeks. Aaronson's pills had started to kick in by then. She told me this would take a while.

I did, in fact, feel better. I began playing squash again with my usual competitiveness, and my concentration improved, and my appetite was returning. I slept more soundly and stopped hoping I'd die in my sleep. In the course of those three weeks I only cried once. Even so, I eagerly awaited his return.

We chatted, and I asked about his vacation. He sounded pleased when I told him I was starting to feel more or less human.

"I don't think I'll need to see you for much longer," I told him after our small talk, "but I know there's still unfinished business. Not just about Sylvester, although I'm not sure exactly what it is."

"Well, for starters you might approach it this way. Suppose you tell me more about what you got from Sylvester that you didn't get from other cats you had?"

I considered. "Most likely that relates to how he felt about *me*. I was special to him. Yolanda usually came home from work before me. She told me he used to come into the living room and wait in the front hall when he heard me open the garage door. And something else—we'd be outside, and I'd call for him and clap my hands, and he'd jump up into my arms. Every summer I got a patch of poison ivy on my neck and shoulder. He liked to traipse around in our backyard bushes where there's considerable poison ivy. He'd get it on his paws and pass it on to me."

Joel Kramer was impressed. "Jumping into your arms . . . that's quite something, for a cat."

"I thought so too." I paused and took a deep breath. There were things I hadn't broached yet, and I knew it wouldn't be easy to go into them. "Sylvester helped me through a very bad time," I said slowly.

"Go on."

"Several years ago, my life turned into a shit storm. Three things happened within the same eight or nine months. Any one of them would have been bad enough, but the combination of all of them pushed me into a blackness I'd never known before."

Another deep breath. "The first thing, my mother died. COVID. She was getting on, she'd just turned 77, and she was obese and hypertensive. Three big risk factors right there. She also had diabetes, which she never took as seriously as she should have. A smart woman but a terrible patient, or at least an incredibly obstinate one. She ate what she pleased, took meds haphazardly, adopted a kind of malignant fatalism. *Whatever happens happens.* I'm not sure she wanted to go on living. The fights with my father, Franny's drinking, Zeke's autism: They all took their toll. Not an easy woman but I loved her and I missed her. Still do.

"The second thing concerns Marisol, my stepdaughter. She's a great kid, and we've gotten very close. I told you she has cystic fibrosis. How much do you know about it?"

"Not a lot. It's genetic, and it mainly involves the lungs. It's very serious."

I nodded. "You can treat it, to a point, but there's no cure. The biggest dangers are repeated pulmonary infections that lead to respiratory failure. Shortness of breath, wheezing, and coughing up blood are some of the major ones, but you can have almost any pulmonary symptoms. I don't know if it's still true, but the average life expectancy for CF patients used to be only 47. That's a terrible black cloud hanging over you, to know you'll quite possibly outlive your child. Yolanda majored in Spanish but went back to school to become a respiratory therapist after she graduated, in order to take care of her. Well, after my mother died, Marisol got pneumonia caused by Pseudomonas, a particularly bad complication. She almost died. We were terrified she'd get COVID, which would have finished her off, no question."

"It must have been a nightmare."

"It was." We fell silent. "The third thing is the most difficult one to talk about," I said finally. "Guillermo Castillo is Yolanda's ex. Marisol's father. A rising star in one of the major telecommunications companies. Guillermo had brought Marisol home one Sunday evening after they'd spent the weekend together. I'd gone to Florida to see my father, who was surprisingly broken up when my mother died. Maybe I shouldn't have been surprised, maybe their fighting was the most intimate thing they had going for them." I fell silent again.

"You were in Florida," Kramer prodded me.

"This was in August . . . very hot . . . Yolanda and Guillermo had a beer. Which turned into two, and then three. He stayed the night. *In our bed.*"

I slammed my fist into the arm of the chair, stood up, paced a bit, and sat down again. "Interesting, how you can know and not know something at the same time. When I came back from Florida, Yolanda was different. Preoccupied, didn't talk much, had trouble with eye contact. I asked her repeatedly what was wrong. The answers were always vague. Problems at work. Or her father was having memory problems, and she wondered if he had early onset dementia. Or Marisol was depressed about something but wouldn't tell her what. I tried to believe her . . . sometimes I did and sometimes not. I've always been uneasy about Guillermo; I thought Yolanda still liked him too much for comfort. Divorce was his idea, not hers. She was on the rebound when we met. Good-looking, good sense of humor, kind of a charismatic bastard. He must make at least three times what I do. Then she told me what *really* happened."

"What did you do?"

"I yelled at her, called her names, drank. Three or four shots of Irish. That's a huge amount for me, I'm not much of a drinker. Then I drove around for most of the night. I'm sure I was over the limit, but I had to get away from her, didn't know what I'd have done if I'd stayed there. Only time I've ever driven drunk."

"How are things between you and her now?"

"Okay, I guess. I don't think about it very often. I love Yolanda even though I don't like her as much as I used to. I've forgiven her . . . I think I have . . ."

Crossing and uncrossing my legs, I shifted my weight but couldn't find a comfortable position. "It doesn't make much sense, but what kept me going throughout all this, more than anything else, was Sylvester. He was even more attached to me than usual; he wouldn't leave me. It's irrational, but it's as if *he knew*. Knew how lousy I felt, knew every day was just another pointless ordeal to get through. I'd watch TV, mostly unaware of what I was watching, and he'd sit next to me. Sometimes he put a paw on my knee. Cats aren't supposed to do things like that, but *he* did."

I thought I could make it through a session dry-eyed for once. Not so.

In our next three meetings, I barely mentioned Sylvester. There was no shortage of other things to talk about. Things that hadn't been on my agenda, at least consciously. More about my mother's death, and my father's emotional absenteeism, and my ungratifying siblings. More about my chronic dissatisfaction with my job but my inability to come up with an alternative. Going to a Caribbean medical school and becoming a doctor when I was pushing 50? Buying a frozen yogurt franchise? Joining the French Foreign Legion? A great idea except that I don't know French and hate violence. Does it even exist anymore?

Then came what I thought would be our final session.

"Last night I dreamt about him," I began.

"Oh?"

"A simple dream, not much of a storyline. Sylvester was sitting on someone's lap. You couldn't see his face, just his lap, but you could tell he was a huge and extremely powerful . . ." I couldn't find the right word. "Entity," I said finally. "An extremely powerful entity. Powerful but benevolent. He wore a flowing white robe. Sylvester made himself completely at home there, purring away to beat the band."

"What do you make of it?" asked Kramer.

"You don't have to be Freud to figure that one out. It was God. Sylvester was on God's lap."

I took a few moments and gazed out of Kramer's window. A cloudless day in early November, a few stubborn leaves still on the trees. "Thing is, I'm not sure if I believe in God. How could He exist, but on the other hand, how could He not? But if He *does* exist, why would He care about one cat and one grieving cat owner in the great scheme of things? Surely He has bigger fish to fry."

"I suppose you'd have to ask him. Hmm, you don't know if you believe in God, but it sounds as if you wish you could."

"I wish I could do all kinds of things." I sounded snippy, for no obvious reason. "I wish I could fly a jet, and pitch the seventh game in the World Series for the Red Sox. I wish I could spend a week in Monaco with Ana de Armas." Kramer gave me a quizzical look. "She's the actress who played Marilyn Monroe in that movie, *Blonde*."

We talked more about the dream, and about Sylvester. We talked more about my marriage, and Marisol. And we talked about something I'd never broached with anyone, apart from Yolanda herself, the question of having another child. We'd both wanted one at times, just not at the same time.

The session came to an end, and I told Kramer I didn't think I'd need another one. But I asked him if he'd see me again if that changed. He said he would, to my relief.

We got another cat a few months later, a female Maine coon, gray with black trim. Skittish—she got along with the three of us but shied away from everyone else who came to the house, scurrying under a bed or to the back of a closet. Feistier than Sylvester, playful but given to scratching us if we dared to play with her too long. Given to throwing up in the living room, her favorite site. The color of her hairballs worked nicely with our expensive plush carpeting. Marisol insisted on naming her Annabel. She'd been studying the works of Edgar Allan Poe, and she loved his poetry.

I like Annabel well enough. She has a good disposition as a rule, she has a great purr, and she's quite beautiful. I think Maine coons are the most attractive felines. Her main flaw: She's not Sylvester, which isn't her fault.

I still think about Sylvester often, and it no longer makes me more than passingly sad. His photo occupies a place of honor on my desk. He's in good company; the only other one is of Yolanda and Marisol at the beach, both of them tanned and smiling.

The memories I have of him are mainly gladdening. I remember him keeping me company while I did my back exercises on the floor, and his putting a paw on my knee while I watched TV, and his jumping into my arms on summer days in our backyard. Never will I feel the same about another cat, not if we have a dozen more. I haven't had more dreams about him, but I often find myself recalling the one I did have— Sylvester, with his eyes half-closed like a luxuriating potentate, purring his way through eternity as he sat on the lap of the God, whom I may or may not believe in.

Volume Control
Aubrey Rebecca

You wouldn't know I was dying—that was the point.

I had a good job, two dogs, and an MBA. I married my high school sweetheart. We lived in a cute downtown apartment.

I was a disco ball spinning over the bar, reflecting everyone else's light. Impossible to look at too closely.

There was Death inside me, and it was a full-time job to keep it tucked away, hidden.

Death, how I know it, is a sludge—putrid, expanding, greedy. I tried to drown it, but it swelled like a sponge, consuming me.

The insidious thing about dying is that you rarely know it is happening. At first, it feels like life.

Then one day you wake up, startled by the stench, and ask yourself, "When did all this sludge get in here?"

That was me.

I share my story because I was dying, but I didn't die.

Not everyone is so lucky.

People want to know why Death found you.

They love to hear you suffered very specific, horrible things that drew Death to you. It reassures them that they are safe.

It allows them to think, "My father didn't [insert horrible thing here], so. Death won't come for me."

It leads to a sick fascination with hearing other people's most painful moments.

I find this obsession with others' grief to be unseemly, so it will suffice to say: my childhood was painful—the Death of a parent, neglect, and abuse.

But these aren't prerequisites for Death.

Back when I was dying, I could name things that had not happened to me, that happened to others. This made me different from those people who were dying, you see.

It turns out I was not.

I was dying just the same.

Perhaps you are dying too.

I'll show you my Death, then you show me yours.

Death wears many faces—it is the original Hecatoncheires, a hundred-handed, fifty-faced being. It is monstrous, but dogged, almost loyal in its pursuit of your demise.

I do not want to minimize Death by calling it one thing— alcoholism, bulimia, codependency.

Each is a head on Death's body; forces of chaotic power striving and straining against one another, with one another.

It was all of them, and none.

"But, Aubrey," I can hear you thinking, "if we cannot name Death and its origins in specific detail, how can I justify how different my life is?"

Or perhaps you know Death is swelling inside you, so instead you ask,

"But, Aubrey, if you cannot name the cause of Death, am I destined to die?"

To answer you both, in no particular order, no.

Of course, you want a sordid tale—arrests, bar fights, and DUIs. I can see you champing at the bit for my family to have stopped speaking to me or for my marriage to have fallen apart.

Unfortunately for you, my story has none of those tales.

I was what they once called "a high-functioning alcoholic," which just meant that alcohol so consumed every second of my day that I contrived my entire life around making sure that people did not consider me a drunk, despite being, well, a drunk.

Most days, this looked like waking up, excelling at my job with a raging hangover, and then cracking my first drink the moment I got home from the office, the wash of bubbles carrying me through the night, one after another, until I collapsed in bed.

I didn't realize I was doing it. That's what was scary. Still is.

I told myself, "If I get a DUI, I'll know I have a drinking problem." Then I built a life designed to prevent a DUI.

I lived within walking distance of pubs and hosted, rather than attended, parties.

Gold star to me! No DUIs here!

The self-trickery continued when I applied to MBA programs at 23. I chose a less rigorous program under the guise of wanting work-life balance. What I meant by work-life balance, however, was the ability to still black out three to four times per week without my degree or job interrupting.

I graduated with a strong GPA, and I did not forgo a single blackout.

Win. Motherfucking win.

I told myself, "An alcoholic could never get their MBA."

Desperate to continue to appear successful, I became a yoga teacher and taught yoga almost every day.

Then, I signed up for a half marathon.

"Alcoholics can't run half marathons," I reassured myself internally, while externally telling anyone who would listen, "I get 13 beers after running 13 miles."

Sometimes, two things can be true. This wasn't one of those times.

In the pursuit of visible success, I decided I needed to be married by 25. I pressured my boyfriend to propose; we were drunk and fighting in the days before he gave me the ring.

Transparently, we were drunk and fighting all the time.

We had started dating at 18, but we fell in love when we started drinking together in college. Our relationship was an incessant ménage à trois with booze. We loved one another, but for a long time, we both loved booze more.

I thought marriage would change us, a magic wand waved over all our hurt and poor communication. Instead, we continued, blacked out at 6 p.m., screaming over dog food and disappointment.

After we had drunkenly called off the wedding earlier in the year, we were down to the wire on my being a 25-year-old bride, but I did it.

I blacked out every day of our minimoon in the name of celebrating our marriage. The fighting continued.

I cried and took rage walks around the block, feeling victimized even when I couldn't remember why we were fighting.

I had to start taking notes on my phone during our fights because my husband was catching on that with a brief distraction, I would lose the thread.

I would check my phone mid-fight, or the next morning, and shake my head, enraged. "Poor Sweet Aubrey," I would tell myself.

But those were not my words; they were the words of Death, of codependency.

I called my boss when I first learned about codependency.

She had previously asked about my obsessive need for her validation. She had asked if I might stop sending her emails about every single task I did. I just wanted her to love me.

I stopped sending so many emails, but burned every time I did something and didn't tell her. I thought this definition of codependency—losing oneself to other people's moods and behaviors in the name of love and acceptance—would interest her.

"Do you have a codependent relationship with people?" she asked, southern drawl ringing through my headset.

"I think I am codependent with every single person I have ever met."

This was the first life truth I ever told.

Years later, my AA sponsor verified I was, in fact, codependent with every person I had ever met. My fourth step—my list of resentments—was 128 people long.

These people had largely wronged me with small transgressions—see: the boy who would bring a single serving of rice to "share" at each potluck dinner.

Ever the codependent, I tried to imply what I wanted, to use my behavior to change people's moods, to change their actions. Ineffective manipulation could have been my middle name.

These days, I put end times on invitations, and if people stay too long, I say, as politely as possible, "Can you please get out of my fucking house?"

I didn't know how to do that back then, when Death was running the show.

Instead, I lived always slighted. I had all this childhood trauma. And a husband, who drank too much and sometimes peed on the bedroom floor and never loaded the dishwasher. Plus, work was stressful.

Codependency was loyal, never canceling on me for drinks, always there to pat my back. It would soothe me while my head rested on the rim of the toilet on a Wednesday night. While I cried, it whispered.

"Sweet girl, you don't deserve all this." All while it bound my hands behind my back.

It left me powerless in the face of my own misery.

And miserable I was—despite all the trappings of the life I had hoped would bring happiness. I'd sit on a paddleboard, or write a poem at sunrise (because alcoholics couldn't wake up at 5:45), and think, "I believe it is all supposed to feel more beautiful than this."

Disco balls are shiny, but they are hollow inside.

I was adorning my Death with glittery eye shadow and fancy rings rather than fighting against it—Death is scarier when it's all dressed up.

I disguised my Death in cheap champagne, popped each Saturday at 8 a.m. in the name of brunch and an ironic DARE T-shirt at the club.

All that sparkle makes it hard to call Death what it is. I was disguising Death from myself. But the heads kept roaring, the hands kept clawing into the dirt, digging me deeper, deeper, deeper.

You can see how codependency and addiction worked together. Remember, there are 48 more heads, all those hundred hands.

Life equips you with a single sword you don't know how to use at first. The hands—your poor decisions, unhelpful beliefs—have to go before you can reach a head. Each cut makes more space for life. Life galvanizes you to keep fighting.

I like to imagine I have cut off about 50 hands, at least 12 heads by now.

The cup is half full. Death is half . . . dead.

My sword swings were the smallest decisions, one stacking on top of another, building me a stepladder out of the life those hands had dug. They say rock bottom is wherever you choose to stop digging, which is true. I think you can also keep digging toward the bottom and building your ladder to freedom in the same breath.

Perhaps you are doing the same.

So how did I first learn to swing my sword at the Hecatoncheires?

It started with a glass of water. Each morning, I would wake up, bleary-eyed and hungover beyond belief at 5:45, for the aforementioned reasons, and I would make myself a cup of coffee. Every health source will tell you the worst way to start your morning is with straight coffee. They tell you to drink a glass of water.

I thought, perhaps, I could fill my coffee cup with water and drink it while the coffee brewed. Come to think of it, I could also take those vitamins that my mom had been asking me to take for years. Plus, I reasoned, maybe this would stop my hands shaking in the morning.

I was 27 and googled "shaking hands in the morning, NOT alcohol" at least twice a month.

Perhaps a glass of water would also ease some of the debilitating anxiety I woke with every day. A psychiatrist had told me he couldn't out-medicate my drinking to fix my anxiety.

He was a fucking quack, anyway. Water and vitamins would fix me.

As small as it was, as misguided as it was. It was my first moment of choosing life. I was writing a new life, swinging my sword at the old one.

I began to read again, having been a voracious reader until college. I discovered a love for memoirs and, without meaning to, I read several sober memoirs in a row. I saw myself in the authors, but it didn't deter me from drinking.

I carried my books to sports bars, where my husband and his friends watched football. I drank my beer and read my book until the page swam in front of me.

It was imperfect, but I was becoming stronger with my sword. It made me wonder what it would be like to actually fight for my life.

The first time I brandished my sword was in November 2021. I realized that, perhaps, my husband and I were not enemies. We were just wasting a lot of energy fighting one another when we could be fighting against whatever was trying to kill us both.

The therapist didn't ask us to stop fighting, though, to be fair, we were on our best behavior with her, diluting our issues during our Zoom sessions. Instead, she had us share our "love meter" each day paired with an ask.

"My love meter is at 5. It would help if we had a night in together. I am feeling lonely."

"Love meter" was a laceration on the face of codependency. It made me rip my cuticles and blush with shame, but it made me name my experience. No longer could I hide behind manipulation and passive-aggressive words. I had to say exactly what I wanted.

Shockingly, when I used my words, the people around me gave me fewer reasons to be resentful. I began to wonder what other words I could use to change my reality.

I started journaling. I began naming my problems and finding solutions.

Solutions looked like lots of burritos, walks, and really long emails to my therapist.

Still. I drank.

For years, when I was particularly drunk, I'd ask my husband if he thought we were alcoholics. Without fail, he'd say, "Yes, babe."

That was the worst answer. It made me cry until I dry-heaved. I needed that to stop.

I thought being an alcoholic was the worst thing I could be.

I told my friends I was going to get sober, anyway. I found Zoom AA meetings and got a Zoom sponsor. My friends told me I was being extreme; we all liked to drink.

I drank every few days.

I dropped out of Zoom AA within the month. I told my sponsor there was no chance I was an alcoholic; my life was so perfect, so manageable.

Instead, I downloaded an app that pinged me every Sunday, asking me to set dry days and a drink limit. I started small: one dry day a week. Five drinks a day during the week. Seven on weekends.

I set the app's "final goal" to the CDC recommendation for women: seven drinks per week. I laughed when I typed it in.

I was drinking 70.

I just wanted to feel normal, to be someone who didn't end her night crying or vomiting. I figured if I could just get the volume of alcohol I was consuming reduced, everything would sort itself out. All that sludge would disappear. I would have saved myself.

I treated it like a math equation—less input would earn me a better output.

The app worked. My drinking dropped 60 percent in a year. Then 90 percent in two. Even though I still felt the pull to drink more, I held steady at five to ten drinks per week. I told myself I was fine. Progress, right?

I was doing things. I was drinking less. I was fighting less. Life looked better. So why did I still feel . . . empty?

With less alcohol flooding me at all times, I could suddenly hear the gremlin that had been living inside me—a voice that watched how much everyone else drank and whispered, More. More. More. I held him off, this mouthpiece of Death.

Every Thursday night, my husband and I fought. I'd come home from cornhole league at the brewery, annoyed at my restraint.

"Why do we always fight on Thursdays?" I asked.

He didn't hesitate. "Because you get drunk every Thursday, Aubrey."

I told him I didn't drink that much—two or three drinks. I was proud of how I had held the gremlin at bay. He shrugged. "But it's enough."

I couldn't argue, and it made me want to die.

On my final blackout, I was in the front yard, holding my neighbor's newborn daughter, looking into her face. Then nothing. Darkness. I don't remember handing her back. I don't remember walking inside.

That moment should have been enough. But even then, I rationalized. It took me three more weeks to get sober.

On my final night drinking, I only had two beers, light beers, not my usual 10 percent IPAs. I was miserable because I wasn't in the arcade with my friends; I was inside, wrestling the gremlin with all my strength. I was furious at not letting myself drink more.

I felt insane.

The next morning, I checked out a different kind of book from the library. Not a memoir. A manual. One that suggested taking a 30-day break from drinking.

I texted a friend to see if she'd do it with me. She laughed. "God, no." I did it anyway.

At first, I just wanted to hit 30 days. I felt morally superior to the old me.

I wore a mental crown that flashed "I am better than you" at my husband, who was still drinking.

As day 30 approached, I panicked. I didn't want to start drinking again. But I also didn't want to call myself an alcoholic. I was only 29. Could a 29-year-old even be an alcoholic? (After a suicide attempt at 19, doctor told me to go to AA. I had ignored them and their medically supported nonsense that you can be an alcoholic at any age.)

I kept not drinking and didn't label myself.

On day 59, May 31, 2023, I went to my first AA meeting—not because I thought I needed it, but because I thought my husband did. Codependency purred inside me—what a good martyr wife I was.

That's when I found out I was an alcoholic.

I got my 24-hour chip and my one-month chip at that first meeting. I went back the next day for my two-month chip.

My husband kept drinking.

I kept not drinking.

Life moved forward in uneven steps.

A few months later, he quit, saying he missed his favorite drinking buddy.

Then, a few months after that, he started again. He didn't like AA. He didn't like the label.

I worried we'd get divorced. I thought about bringing home a bottle of tequila and taking shots until things were right again.

I was at the gym when the thought occurred to me. Wall balls and deadlifts have a way of eliminating every thought in your head. I was too tired to drive to the package store when I left. (My out-of-state friends do not believe me that this is what we call liquor stores in Connecticut. Google it; I didn't make this up.)

I didn't drink. I hoped for a magical solution.

I waited for the lightning bolt, but the magic didn't come. Not in the big prophetic way I wanted.

It came from the tiny decisions, the incremental steps that I took to walk into a new life. It helped that I had to walk five miles a day in early sobriety to manage my anxiety and all this energy I wasn't burying under alcohol.

I can say I built the ladder out of my misery faster when I wasn't spending half my time digging myself deeper. I slew four of the Hecatoncheires' heads.

I found that it wasn't about decreasing the volume of alcohol I was drinking; it was about turning up the volume on my life. It was that I hadn't been able to hear the pulse and pull of my life under the roar of the beer.

I built a life the only way I could, one decision at a time.

I kept reading, writing, learning tarot.

I started a skincare routine.

I went on an antidepressant.

My life got louder, fuller.

I joined a gym. (Is CrossFit a cult? Maybe.)

I ran a half marathon.

I ate a donut and drank a Diet Coke at the finish line. I drank zero beers after running 13 miles. I was slow, my legs hurt, but I smiled through the entire race. I was joyful. My husband cried at the finish line because he was so proud. Also, maybe because he was sleep-deprived. He had driven me to the race bus at 4:30 a.m.

Life had multiplied and expanded, eclipsing the space available for Death. I had added life back into my days. It's incredible how much time you have for life when you're not drinking in front of the TV ten hours a day. Now, I only turn on the TV to do the *New York Times* crossword with friends. I couldn't do that drunk—sometimes we barely manage it sober.

My husband got sober again.

I manage my resentments before they bloom.

I only let the voice call me "Sweet Baby Aubrey" when the gym or the run was too hard. Or sometimes when my husband loads the dishwasher wrong.

I held my grandmother's hand every day until she died, sober and without yoking my wellness to her physical decline.

I am on a slow, compounding journey out of my old life, out of that old reality.

That life was a dark living room, the glow of the television, and an empty six-pack at my feet.

I exchanged one moment for another until they added up to this life.

Today, it's not about what external things have changed. I still sit on my paddleboard, watch the sunrise, and journal, but now it's for more than the camera in my hand.

In making this new life, I've built something worth defending, worth picking up my sword for.

I am not dying anymore insofar as there is more life than sludge. I am unburdened, relieved. Even amidst health concerns, life stress, and my nana's passing, I have found inordinate joy. I could not have had both. I needed to slay the many heads and hands of Death.

I needed to free myself, one cut at a time, from its grip.

I hold my sword in one hand and a Diet Coke in the other. My grandmother lived to be 95. She used to put Diet Coke in my baby bottle because she loved it so much. With her genes and soda affinity, I have a lot of years left to fight this Death beast.

I am ready.

Turn the volume up.

SINCERELY, SARAH
Nikita Costiuc

I caught him scrolling through pages of Romanian baby names.

Not baby names. Not Eastern European baby names. Romanian baby names.

"What are you looking at, Jake?"

He snapped his laptop shut. "DND stuff. Picking a character name."

I nodded, like that made sense.

We used to kiss each other goodnight and spend weekends in bed, sipping caramel macchiatos with extra whipped cream. Now we slurped SpaghettiOs, discussed comedy podcasts, and scheduled goodnight texts from the couch.

Pink champagne goes flat after a few years, they said, and insanity won't bring the bubbles back. But pages of Romanian baby names and a sudden DND obsession could only mean one thing: My husband had made a baby with someone else, someone Romanian.

I screamed into a bathroom towel like any sane woman would after discovering her husband's Romanian baby, then circled back over dinner. "Tell me about this stuff."

He talked with his mouth full. "SpaghettiOs? They're delicious."

"DND stuff. How often do you 'stuff' her?"

He licked his lips and dug his spoon back into the bowl. "Not sure what you mean, but I'd love to play DND with you."

Pervert.

I took deep breaths. "Is DND delicious?"

A noodle clung to his chin as his spoon hovered. "In a way, yes."

"Who is she?"

He frowned and gulped another scoop. "Who?"

"Romanian DND."

"Oh! It's a 'he' actually: a knight named Catalin. Awesome name, right?" He grinned, shoving more SpaghettiOs into his mouth.

He enjoyed torturing me, but I wouldn't give him the satisfaction. I confronted him again that night as he brushed his teeth. "Tell me about your Romanian baby."

He spit a stream of white foam. "What?"

I turned off the faucet and grabbed his toothbrush. "You fathered a Romanian baby."

His mouth opened, but nothing came out, like his brain was still buffering.

I jabbed his chest. "Oscar-worthy performance. You should've been an actor, not an engineer."

He tilted his head as his gaze flicked around the room. "This about DND?"

"That's what we're calling your side piece?"

He backed away, hands up. "Sarah, there's no Romanian baby, trust me."

I did trust him, but as Ronald Reagan said, trust but verify.

I developed a routine.

Midnight—grab his phone and lock myself in the bathroom.

Password? Took a few weeks, but I figured it out: 1d20.

I studied every message and app but found only DND group chats, movie trailers, and memes. The memes didn't look Romanian, but I wasn't an expert yet.

He forgot to delete his boss's texts, though, the ones that came at 12 p.m. and read, "Where are you?"

Not proof, but a crack.

I needed more, so I slapped a tracker on his car. After a month, I realized my mistake: His calling was spying, not acting. His car traced the same route—work, home, work, home—except on Fridays, when he claimed to play DND at the library.

The best lies are 90 percent truth, and while the final 10 percent always reveals itself (babies, after all, get born), I'd married a gold medal cheater. For a full year, he juggled his job, his Romanian mistress, and their Romanian baby while keeping the same routine and receiving the same 12 p.m. texts: *Where are you?*

Still, I was willing to forgive. I just wanted the truth, an apology, not this silent torture.

My parents shook their heads. "Honey, he's probably just playing DND."

My so-called friends lectured me on boundaries, projection, and intrusive thoughts.

The private investigator dismissed me. "No evidence of any sexual partner, Romanian or otherwise."

"Did you check for secret cars? Offshore accounts? Disguises?"

"Sweetie, your husband leads a boring life: just work, home, and DND."

I slammed my fist on his desk. "You needed to prove that 'DND' meant 'doing a Romanian.'"

Instead of a refund, he handed me a therapist's card, so I left a one-star review.

Like most things in life, if you want it done right, do it yourself. Over another SpaghettiOs dinner, I made my move. "Jake, can I join your DND group?"

His eyes widened as he fumbled with his spoon. "Of course."

He rambled the whole way there about plot twists and character arcs.

At the library, I pounced, rushing to the front desk. "Sorry, stupid question. Is there a DND group here?"

"Over there," the clerk said.

From inside the meeting room, a man in a ridiculous hat shouted at my husband. "Catalin, no more spells."

My husband waved a foam sword. "No promises, Ramron."

They were all oblivious, even the clerks.

I jumped on a table and flung a stack of spellbooks at my husband. "Admit it. You're sleeping with a Romanian."

"Sarah, this again? There's no Romanian."

"Then why specifically Romanian baby names?"

"Because they're cool. Catalin is an awesome name."

The clerk approached, but I didn't flinch. "I have proof," I said. "Open your phone."

He handed it over, and I pulled up his boss's texts. "Twelve p.m. Every week. Explain that."

He closed his eyes, then lied again. "It's the end of lunch. He texts us if he doesn't see us at our cubicles."

The court deemed what happened next "excessive," which I won't dispute, but it was understandable at the time, given the circumstances.

Prosecutors dropped the assault and battery charge in exchange for anger management classes.

The library ban was silly.

The divorce was equitable: I got my peace—he kept everything else.

I moved to an apartment and developed a fondness for hunting remotes and bottles near the couch. My parents offered to cover some of the rent if I saw a therapist, which I did because I needed the help (financial, not mental). The therapist responded to my story with, "That sounds difficult." In one session, she asked if there were any Romanian babies in the room with us. I quit soon after and paid rent by cashiering at a department store.

One Thursday afternoon, a woman came to my register with a toddler in her cart.

My jaw hurt from a day of forced smiles, but I had a streak going, so I bared my teeth as I scanned her items. "How are you?"

"I am good." Her voice was accented.

"Find everything okay?"

She patted her toddler's head. "We have everything we need, don't we, Catalin?"

Sweat trickled down my back. I jammed the buttons, muttered the total without looking up, and shoved the receipt across the counter.

She grabbed my hand. "Your husband is waiting."

My ears rang. My throat tightened. My hand burned as if branded.

I don't remember what the customers said or what my manager yelled. I only remember running after her—and finding Jake, my boring husband, smiling outside.

"Sarah, don't be shy. I'll waive the restraining order."

I pointed to his Romanian baby and his Romanian mistress. "Why?"

He snorted. "Look at yourself. You're a housewife in every sense, except cooking. The only edible thing we had were SpaghettiOs."

I blinked hard. "How?"

He picked up his toddler and smiled. "We used her car. Your PI missed that, didn't he?"

"PI?"

He rolled his eyes. "Sarah, you thought you were the only one reading texts? Good catch with my boss, by the way. I forgot about those, but I recovered quickly, didn't I?"

I glanced at her, then back at him. "DND?"

He laughed and ruffled the hair of his Romanian baby. "An excuse to leave the house until you caught me picking a name for Catalin and forced me to join a real geek group."

He shook his head. "Learning critical hits, spell slots, and damage modifiers from Ramron? Cruel."

My knees buckled. "Why not just ask for a divorce?"

"And hand you half of my assets? Split the house you never cleaned, the investments you didn't pick? No, thank you. I needed a parachute that got me out with most of my stuff and left you in a pile of burned, twisted metal."

He grinned at his Romanian baby. "I wasn't sure how to pull it off, but then I saw you in the bathroom with my phone. I thought Romanian baby hunting would drive you insane, but even I didn't expect such a perfect finale. By tackling me, you shared the answer key with the entire class."

He waved a finger. "Still, I paid a price, sneaking around with foam swords and costumed imbeciles. Because of you, Sarah, I listened to more of Ramron's gibberish than my own child's. But it was worth it: In the end, no one will believe we had this conversation."

He strapped his Romanian baby into the car seat and slid into the front. His Romanian mistress sat beside him, her face lowered. Exhaust circled the air as he started the engine.

"Her uncle hired me, so we're moving to Romania. Everything's cheaper there, except life insurance. But you deserved a proper goodbye."

As they pulled out of the parking lot, she gave me a quiet nod, and I watched my husband with his Romanian mistress and their Romanian baby drive out of my life.

No one believed me, Jake was right about that. I went back to the register and the couch. Eventually, to keep my eyeballs from becoming SpaghettiOs, I wandered out to the park, where, of course, I met you.

When you stretched out your hand, and I recoiled, you didn't make that face: You said I didn't have to shake it if I didn't want to. You smiled and said hello even when I didn't respond. You said that you also enjoyed reality TV. And you brought me caramel macchiatos with extra whipped cream.

You're reading this because yesterday, you asked me to be your girlfriend, and I thought maybe you'd believe me if I wrote it all down.

And if you don't, then I hope you die in a fire.

No, I'm kidding.

You're special, and I owe you honesty.

Here it is.

I feel safer when people stand three feet away from me than beside me. I twitch around babies, and my family tells me about every new mental health facility. But you've shown me life outside of all that. With you, I feel safe, even in the SpaghettiOs aisle.

You've asked for my heart. Pieces of it are stuffed in couch cushions, hidden in bathroom towels, and crushed under library tables. But what's left is still beating, and it's yours. Just promise to play board games with dice, not secret cars, stab me with foam swords in the front, not the back, and name your Romanian babies together with me.

Sincerely,

Sarah.

A Marvelous Thread of History: An Epic Treasure Hunt

Captain Blake

There are very few experiences more satisfying for an old sailor and diver with a sense of maritime history than to find an ancient shipwreck. If that discovery is the direct result of long research in dusty archives in the depth of an English winter, and if that shipwreck lies, in pleasant contrast, in the warm, limpid waters of a Southeast Asian coral reef; and further, if that wreck is discovered after weeks of laborious survey work, then a sense of pleasurable accomplishment complements the satisfaction. If there follow months of arduous underwater work in excavating the bones of the wreck from deep within its coralline burial site, that feeling of accomplishment is further enhanced. Supposing, just supposing, mind you, that the wreck yields treasure worth millions of brass razoos, then the satisfied, accomplished old sailor might even feel a slight spasm of pecuniary elation. But such a crass emotion has nothing to do with this story. In fact that mendacious nerve never even twitched. What this particular wreck did yield was an electrifying historical experience, one as close to travel back in time as is possible in these times of mindless, breakneck descent into a slavish future of dependence on electronic gadgets, a future increasingly insensitive to memory of our History, one near devoid of Romance.

This ship was wrecked in September 1789. Our brotherly band of divers and salvors discovered the wreck in 1986, and worked hard during the calm seasons over the next three years, six months of underwater work in all, finding very little of the treasure of 64,000 silver Spanish dollars that should have remained in her bones. It was in September 1989, exactly two hundred years after the wreck, that we found out why our efforts had been unrewarding—in the strictly monetary sense.

A slender thread of historical fact was then finally drawn out, marvelously intact, over two whole centuries, and woven into the fabric of our modern lives, to convince the greedy among us to abandon vile thoughts of riches. Astonishingly, the master weaver at the other end was none other than Captain William Bligh, a name etched indelibly in my consciousness from my schooldays, and a name that any serious moviegoer would recognize from no less than three Hollywood epics that have separately told the tale of the mutiny on board HMS *Bounty*—that greatest true romance of the sea ever enacted.

How such a fragile thread of connection with an improbable past warped into our present lives needs to be explained.

Vansittart **was a full-rigged** ship of the British East India Company—self-styled The Honourable East India Company—the first real British multinational. She was armed with 32 iron 12-pounder cannons (note the magnetic nature of this armament). She was registered as 499 tons gross, but probably displaced more like 830 tons. This deliberate fiction was a device to avoid the legal requirement to carry a chaplain, or "Godbotherer" in 18th century seamen's parlance, on all British ships over 500 tons. Without this subterfuge the *Vansittart*'s robust crew would doubtless have preferred to sail away leaving the Godbotherer gagged and bound to a bollard on the docks of Tilbury, or better still, to heave him into ten fathoms off the Lizard with a cannonball lashed to his ankles. Anyway, God had no place East of Suez, where there ain't no Ten Commandments, and a man can raise a thirst. I believe I would have been happier in the 18th than the 20th . . . and I eschew the 21st completely.

H.E.I.C. Ship *Vansittart* was wrecked "somewheres West of Beringga Island, with 56 chests of Treasure," as was related in the initial, brief, and substantially incorrect account that I saw. This report, geographically vague though it was, proved enough to spark some mild cases of Treasure Fever among my youthful and unworldliwise crew members.

On a subsequent research trip through European archives, I naturally took up the case of the *Vansittart* while in the depths of the India Office, the archives of the H.E.I.C. I gained admittance therein on the strength of several letters of introduction from genuine scholars. I felt a trifle guilty in pursuing sunken treasure under what might have been construed as false pretenses, but my interest in maritime history was genuine, and I pursued many other facets during months of fascinating research work: contemporary shipboard conditions, navigation techniques, and the disdain among seafarers for Religionists of all stripes being some of those.

The last logbook of the *Vansittart* was faithfully preserved in the India Office, after a dramatic escape from the sinking ship, through a long voyage home to a Court of Enquiry, and then painstakingly conserved by generations of librarians.

Here I must pay heartfelt tribute to such librarians and their staff, these literate, extremely well informed, and dedicated guardians of the past. They are very poorly paid, especially when compared to the most lowly Illiterati of the dot.com age, but they perform their mission with zeal.

An aside to illustrate the dedication of one such exemplar, the charming, elderly lady librarian of the India Office: I was reading accounts of an English wreck of 1622 in Indian waters, well before the establishment of the H.E.I.C. Among the list of survivors was one "Mathew Guthrie, Ordinary Seaman." A scrawled postscript in a different hand added that he was "suspected of purloining part of the Treasure" during the escape from the wreck. I was fascinated—might this very Ordinary Seaman have contrived thereby to acquire a minor sultanate in India of his own, complete with harem, on the ill-gotten proceeds? Or perhaps, more likely, to have established a trading godown, destined to become the well-known colonial firm of Guthrie's? My curiosity was further piqued when I later read his name in a list of "Convicts suitable for release to English Ships" in Calcutta, on the other side of India from the wreck, and a bare six months thereafter. Perhaps Matt the convict had been relieved of his share by the authorities? Another contemporary list of "English Ships Arriving and Departing from the Port of Calcutta" was named in the indices and promised further possible information about the fate of Matt Guthrie. I ordered the document for viewing and waited for it to be "brought down from the archives" by the leathery, aging stewards. After a longer wait than usual, the librarian herself appeared, looking quite flustered. She apologized profusely that the list could not be found, exclaiming that "something like this has not happened in years!" How admirable that a guardian of past truth should be so perturbed at the possible loss of such an insignificant, archaic item! One wonders what reception one would receive today for a similar request in Canton, or Moscow . . . or Singapore? I have a dismal answer to the last.

Another digression: Matt Guthrie's appearance in pieces of paper six months apart and four hundred years ago, along with the librarian's fierce defense of such minutiae, suggests that History will never fully be falsified, not by any fascist, communist, or neo-Confucian dictatorship—no government goon, however fanatic, could ever fake such lovingly detailed, dovetailing records!

The logbook of the *Vansittart* was beautifully inscribed in copperplate hand, in articulate detail. She had run onto an uncharted reef, kedged off, and then "cut and run" (the seafaring origin of that phrase), where the anchor cable is veered to one side, usually employing another cable through the quarter gallery windows at the stern. This has the effect of turning the ship's head down wind, or in a safer direction, whereupon some sail is set, both cables are *cut* through simultaneously with axes, and the ship *runs*, or gains way toward safer, deeper water.

The ship was not now safe, however. With six feet of water in the hold, and this increasing despite frantic efforts at the pumps, she was literally sinking under the feet of the crew. The captain chose the only feasible chance of saving his ship: He sailed her as fast as her increasing deadweight allowed "towards the Coast of Beringga Island," where, if he could beach her before she should sink there was a chance that effective repairs might be carried out, the crews' lives saved, and the treasure safeguarded. With this last in mind,

13 of the chests of silver were carried up on deck, as much as they could retrieve before the ingress of water stopped their efforts. They also retrieved "dry powder for the guns, some muskets, and all the bread."

She did not reach the beaches of Beringga. "With ten feet of water in her, in a sinking condition," she was run by the captain onto a reef somewhere off the coast, where she stuck fast. With the gun deck almost awash, and access below cut off, further efforts to bring up the treasure were made by "scuttling the main-deck"—cutting through it with axes and saws—but without success.

"From the Piratical Disposition of the Malays, we cannot expect to remain in peacable possession of the Ship. . . . We could defend Her if she remains intire, yet if she parts asunder, breaks up or heels off, which is to very much apprehended, we could derive no benefit from our Guns, and must fall a Conquest to Numbers. . . . Staying by the Ship will serve to convince the Malays there is an object to preserve, quitting her will delude them."

They "spiked" the guns, hammering a spike into the touch-hole, which without recourse to a gun-founder's workshop, rendered them useless.

They threw the 13 chests of silver over the side "to lessen the possibility of the Malays finding the whole." All this work was accomplished despite "some Drunkenness" on the part of the crew, a common theme in shipwreck stories (see "The Wreck of the Royal Captain").

"With 114 people in the Cutter, Long-boat, Pinnace, Yawl, Jolly-boat and Gig," they sailed 25 leagues to a bay on the north end of the island, where they found two English ships: *Nonsuch*, Captain Canning, and *General Elliot*, Captain Lloyd. The two ships returned to the wreck to find it had been "burned to the waterline by the Malays," probably to more easily extract the iron and bronze nails. Perusal of the logbook of the *Nonsuch* showed drawings of the lead seals that were used to seal the treasure chests.

Over four days the combined crews managed to retrieve 40 chests of silver, which, by a bit of arithmetic, left 16 chests behind in the wreck, each with the standard 4,000 coins— 64,000 Spanish dollars!

The *Vansittart's* logbook offered some clue as to the wreck's location—"a reef off the West Coast of Beringga Island"—but the modern chart shows miles of reef that fit that description. Even during a desperate struggle for the survival of a ship, a well-trained quarterdeck crew will take bearings and transits off known landmarks, sometimes pinpointing a wreck site to within a few hundred meters, but the *Vansittart* was floundering along, on the point of foundering, in completely uncharted waters (no English ship had sailed there before 1789) so the logbook's lack of precise navigational data was forgivable. There seemed little prospect of finding the leveled bones of a wooden sailing ship under miles of ever-expanding coral reef two hundred years after the event. I moved on to different archives in the Greenwich Maritime Museum.

I camped by day for two months in the Reading Room, where a rich diet of original map folios, manuscript "Voiages of Discouery," and sundry travelers' accounts offered what must surely be the ultimate in armchair travel and adventure, but little news of "fhipwrack." For marvelous distraction, and for bodily needs brought on by that rich diet, I would navigate my way to the unheated, dismal "Gentlemen's Toilet" by no less than four different routes, one through the Model Galleries, one through the Navigation Gallery, another through the Marine Arts Hall, and the last by way of the cafeteria. Each of these was a voiage of discovery in itself, there being no less than 72 line items on the cafe's menu. But I digress . . . I had found little about shipwrecks in SE Asia that would help to guide me to a specific Lat and Long. I moved to the Map Room.

The voluminous Index Volumes of the Map Room archives, in themselves an archaeological site, ripe for systematic excavation, offered "A Map of Beringga Island . . . late 18th Century." I had forgotten up to now about the doomed *Vansittart*, but this was worth perusing, although unlikely to yield anything more than the modern charts. At least it was of the right period.

The map emerged from its drawer, where it may well have rested unmolested for most of the last two centuries. It would have been a severe disappointment to a general geographer for despite its grand title it was merely a small sketch of a part of the West Coast with a scattering of islands offshore, but! In fine print, "Vansittart Wrack 1789" lay close to a symbolic shipwreck, in definite relation to a group of islets! I rushed to the modern chart drawers. BA 1149 showed the same group of islets; the wreck symbol on the sketch map, when transposed onto the modern one, lay near the edge of an extensive coral reef. Now the ultimate fate of the *Vansittart* lay open to further, modern investigation!

By now it was 6.30 p.m. on a winter's night in London. The Keeper of Maps, sensing my new interest, had kindly kept the room open for me well behind closing time, but now it was time to leave.

I was ill-prepared, and woefully underclothed, for the freezing sleet, rain drops half frozen, that pelted me as I waited forever for a number 88 bus, huddled under a drooping brolly, but the certain knowledge that the next step in the saga of the *Vansittart* would be played out in the warm, limpid waters of the South China Sea fired an internal glow that almost had me turning cartwheels in the rain-dark, ice-cold street.

Our sturdy ferro-cement ketch *Four Friends* (*Old4F*, as distinct from the Schooner *New4F*), veteran of many wreck-hunting voyages, was equipped with magnetometer and side-scan sonar for "survey work" (i.e., wreck-hunting), plus two road compressors for driving airlifts (great underwater vacuum cleaners), with prop-wash (a great elbow that deflects the wash from the ship's propellor downward), diving compressors, and of course our crew—as scurrilous a set of scoundrels and sea-lawyers as ever sailed the seven seas, serial sacreligionists all.

Four Friends loading gear in a backwater of an Eastern Port. Aft is one of the compressors for airlifting. On top of the helideck is the large elbow for prop-blasting. Captain on gangplank.

Our wreck was almost certainly buried entirely under 197 years of coral growth. Side-scan sonar would show nothing of this, so we deployed the magnetometer along the most likely reef front. A magnetometer "fish," towed some 100 meters behind the survey ship, and sometimes 20 meters deep (in order to avoid that ship's own magnetic field), does little more than measure the precise strength of Mother Earth's field. The trick in wreck-hunting is to recognize distortions in the maternal field caused by magnetic anomalies, in this case, we hoped, by those 32 iron cannons carried by *Vansittart*, our target.

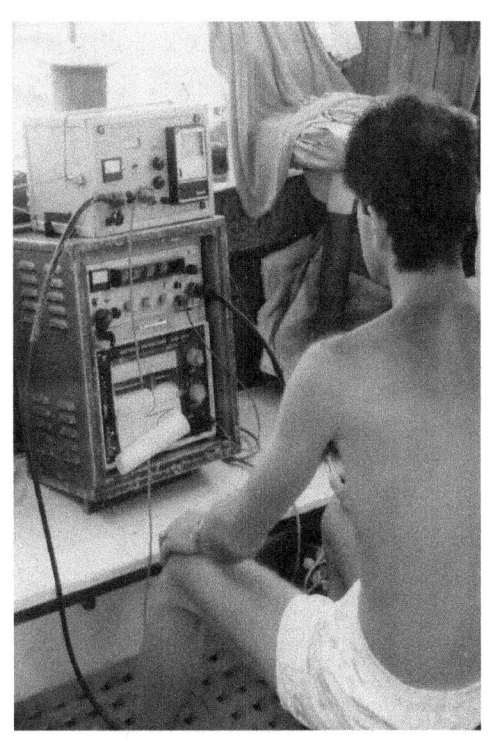

As always, the "most likely target reef" showed a steady 41,600 gammas, no anomalies, just coral reef, a benign growth on the belly of dear old Mum.

Hardened to such disappointments by previous months of survey work to find just one wreck, we prepared a systematic survey, in which the likeliest areas are successively eliminated beyond doubt, and so on.

After a week of patient work, a great "Yahoo!" from the man at the mag signaled a spike on the trace of 150 gammas to the right, with an abrupt crossover to 80 gammas left. Since the reef front lay to starboard, we could be sure our "anomaly," not yet our "wreck," lay on the reef to starboard of where the magnetometer fish was tracking at the time of the anomalous trace. We anchored, and all went swimming. Just acres of mostly dead coral, no visible artefact of Man. We kept swimming around, peering into crevices for some linear regularity. Alan, that canniest of wreck ferrets, swung his axe at a tall, thin coral. Layers of growth flaked off, leaving a shiny, yellow-greenish vertical rod—an 18th-century bronze keel-bolt by gosh! We had found our wreck! The beer flowed that night, somewhat prematurely, as it turned out.

Over the next three years, during each calmer season of the SW monsoon, six to eight men labored heavily underwater for a total of six months, removing hundreds of tons of coral, and exposing the keel timbers and floor frames along most of the 118 feet of keel of an 800-ton wooden sailing ship.

This was a huge labor, and before I finally get around to that Marvelous Thread of History that I promised pages ago, I hope the reader will bear with some description of a few highlights of what was almost a classic treasure hunting epic . . . minus the treasure.

By prop-blasting the surface of the reef, which slowly loosens the structure until sand comes spurting out of crevices, and then larger pieces start to flake off, we started the destruction and removal of the dead coral that overlaid the wreck. This was carried out by positioning the ship, with its propellor encased in a huge elbow, precisely over the target spot. Such precision is guided by a "Master-Blaster" who hangs in the water alongside watching the process, and issuing commands such as "Two feet to port!" whereupon deck crew winch the ship in that direction.

The process was continued using the airlifts, 20-foot-long plastic drain-pipes 8 inches in diameter. When compressed air is pumped in great volume into the bottom of these, they become erect and suck sand and coral in the bottom, spewing it out of the top. These vacuum cleaners are capable of voluminous, violent displacement, or by throttling back on the air, of delicate precision, where the diver places the tube nearby and gently fans sand into the opening with his hand, hopefully exposing thereby heaps of silver coins.

When both airlifts were operating at full blast, the underwater scene was one of utter chaos, with roiling clouds of sediments reducing visibility to zero except at the very mouth of the tube. Should a flat piece of coral, or a diver's fin, become sucked in and jammed over the mouth, the tube instantly becomes filled with air only and attempts to rise violently to the surface like a Polaris missile leaving its submarine tube. Now the diver must both exhale sharply, to avoid pulmonary embolism, and must close off the air valve to avoid actually breaking through the sea surface like that Polaris rocket. At this point the tube becomes heavy once more, and darts back down into the swirling maelstrom, with the diver hanging on like a witch on a broomstick, to land goodness knows where, hopefully not on something too sharp, and not on one's fellow divers—all good fun, especially for the old hands on deck watching a new trainee zooming out of the surface and plunging back again and again like an manic pogo-stick all over, and well beyond, the site of the wreck.

In between the mechanized mayhem, all hands would go in to manually clear the site, to move boulders by hand that were far too large for the airlifts. Now coral rock is not massively dense, perhaps only twice as dense as water, so underwater it weighs only half as much. Divers were therefore able to move incongruously huge boulders the size of a small piano, and there was nothing quite so exciting, or alarming, than to run downhill with boots on, not fins, embracing a lump the size of a beanbag, and over which one could not see, across the chaotic, craggy surface of our site, to dump it on the sand flats outside the reef, only to have to hump the same damned lump once or twice again as our site expanded.

All of this quarrying activity exposed most of what was left of the ship, its keel, floor frames, and planking up to the turn of the bilge—all massive oak timbers, seemingly as solid as the day they were hewn, but destined to dry out and rot quickly if exposed to air.

The excavation work also produced a wall of coral rock on the inshore side, which at one point towered near vertical 18 feet above the hull. We had shifted hundreds of tons of coral.

A few artefacts were left among the ship's bones: broken wine bottles, ceramic storage jars, the ship's Traverse Slate for navigation, with its columns and headings scratched in but no actual data; presumably these had been entered in ephemeral chalk. I found a quite modern-looking rubber stamp with the letters of a name attached. The letters appeared confusing underwater, and when cleaned on the surface proved more so. All the letters were there to spell out William Laurence (the second officer according to the logbook, where he was Wm. Laurence), but they were not merely back to front, as is normal, they were also in reverse order. One wonders whether Wm. L. was clever enough to be a responsible officer?

Another extraordinary experience: Just three-quarters of a mile away from our site there was a detachment of Marines, guardians of the coast. Naturally they came initially to inspect us, two of them in a dug-out canoe with their rifles. We saw them coming, hurriedly detached, and deep-sixed every compressed air pipe, every down line, every lifting bag, and covered our steaming compressors with tarpaulins. We all pulled out fishing rods to pretend eccentric fishermen. Our visitors proved real gentlemen, actually helping us to bait our lines effectively, and inviting us to dinner at their camp. We took along several cases of beer, and these convivial exchange visits went on over the three years of our work. Indeed, we swapped Christmas cards with their sergeant for some years thereafter. Our guilt at hiding our real activities from our friends was somewhat assuaged by our failure to find any objects of value; we were just eccentric nutcases after all!

Of the ship's treasure we found just 78 coins, as well as 9 (of the expected 16) lead seals that safeguarded each treasure chest. These had the emblem of the H.E.I.C. stamped into them. Where were the rest of the 63,922 silver dollars that we could have expected to find? Where were all the 32 iron cannons?

At endless discussion and poring over detailed site plans after dinner each night, numerous theories were advanced about there being another portion of the wreck as yet unearthed.

Maybe it lies over there! Captain at left.

To test some of these theories we did a very detailed magnetometer survey of a rectangle 80 m by 50 m around the hull. This clearly showed three large spikes in the variations of the magnetic field—magnetic anomalies. Two of these we had already unearthed, one large anchor and one amorphous iron mass, perhaps the ship's oven. The third anomaly was no larger than these two, so constituted not more than one cannon, not worth excavating. Where were all the cannons?

We had obviously been the first modern salvors (look at all that coral growth!), but was it possible that there had been contemporary fellow looters too? Who in this isolated area would have had the equipment in the late 18th century to carry out such heavy work? And who would bother to salvage rusted iron cannons? Heavy objects of no utility on the light Malay vessels.

We gave up work temporarily, airlifted sand back to cover the hull timbers to preserve them, and sailed back to Singapore.

I found a clear answer to our questions during another research trip to the archives. Back in the Greenwich Museum Reading Room I was privileged to hold, and carefully turn the pages of, the manuscript account by Captain William Bligh of his voyage in one of HMS *Bounty*'s small open boats, the *Launch*, into which he and 18 other loyal crew were roughly bundled at the time of the mutiny. Bligh, against all odds, and certainly against the expectations of the mutineers, safely navigated this cockle-shell of a boat 4,000 miles (7,500 kilometers) to Kupang in Timor, losing only one man.

While he was recuperating in Batavia, modern Jakarta, where in dreadful irony he lost some of his men to diseases, he wrote this in his diary: "9th October, 1789. This day anchored in the Road of Batavia, the English Ship General Elliot, Captain Lloyd, with the survivors of the Hon. East India Co. Ship Vansittart, a wreck on the coast of Beringga. They saved 40 of the 55 [*sic*] chests of the Treasure. One man only was lost in the wreck, and five others in the Gig were missing, who were supposed to have taken some of the Treasure."

So, Bligh found out about the wreck, and the news of treasure remaining therein, a few hours after the survivors arrived! That means the news must have spread like wildfire on the Batavia waterfront, and who else more capable of salvage, then as today, than those clever, swag-bellied Hollanders who propped up the waterfront bars of that hub of the Malay Archipelago? By the next morning there must have been several rival parties fitting out schooners with A-frames to lift heavy cannons aboard, and recruiting sea-gypsies, breath-holding divers, already famous in the pearl-diving industry, to do their underwater work, especially to scoop silver dollars out of chests—and in the process spill at least 78 loose coins.

Now Captain William Bligh, if not quite a hero to me, has always been an influence in my life. I have tried, strutting my own small quarterdeck, to emulate some of Bligh's worst attributes: I have attempted the brutal captain, contemptuous of the feelings of subordinates, but with little effect: no dramatic mutiny—my crews, especially the ladies, ignore my sallies, or threaten to report me to the police, and those crew that are both ladies and family just regard my attempts as "Daddy making noises again!" I dream of aspiring to a magnificent feat of seamanship such as Bligh's open-boat voyage from the mutiny to Timor, but nowadays the sea is littered with sign-posts, intersecting radio waves, and corrupting, effete marinas; and anyway, a voyage in such a tiny, over-crowded boat would be intercepted by various officious coast guards, and subsequently forbidden port clearances by imperious harbormasters . . . Romance is dead, save in the imagination!

But I can think of no more Romantic association with that querulous, stern old Sea Dog than to have him reach out to me, to me personally, across two hundred years, to advise me that those Hollander salvors, my spiritual forbears, had beaten me to the spoils!

Some have said, "What a pity you did not read Bligh before doing all that work!" But I disagree. I would not have missed any aspect of the whole intoxicating process, the dusty archives, the Treasure Fever, the freezing rain, the months of hard physical labor under the tropic sea, and the final entanglement in Bligh's historical thread. Not for all the silver in the ocean!

PS: Captain Bligh mentions that "five of the crew went missing in the Gig, who were supposed to have taken some of the Treasure." What happened to them? Much later I unearthed one clue: In correspondence of India House, London, to Fort William in Calcutta (the Asian HQ of the H.E.I.C), 1790: "you acted very properly in noticing the liberality of the King of Tringano in ransoming five Englishmen, supposed to have been lost in the wreck of the Vansittart."

Now modern Terengganu is 1,000 miles from Beringga! What sort of adventures did the five endure in getting there, in the ship's gig, a tiny open boat? Bligh is alone in recording the suspicion that they had stolen part of the treasure, but there must have been some report circulated at the time. Shades of Matt Guthrie! Note that the "kings" of the Malay coastal sultanates of those days considered it their divine right to any shipwreck, and to enslave any survivors, so what caused the "liberality" of Tringano? He "ransomed" the Englishmen. Who paid whom, one wonders? And did the *Vansittart*'s silver play a part? History can provide tantalizing clues, but it does not explain everything that occurred.

Nocturne

Olivia Bacon

We rattle down the highway at Mach speed
and I, in the bed of the pickup truck, curse
the moron who told me to squeeze next
to these whooping boys. I don't do illegal things,
I tell myself, while the high beams of the following car
illuminate me doing something totally illegal.
Squeezing each other's arms, my friend and I
crouch together. Our sneakers anchor us to the
dusty ridges of the bed. My spine bangs against
the diamond tread of the aluminum tool box
and I spit her hair out of my mouth. We look
at each other and cackle. The boys howl at the
stars, and my eyes rise with their shouts past
the headlights and into new-moon darkness.
Only the cicadas in their sticky circadian rhythms
could tell me how many hours since moonrise, but
the engine growls them out. The world is a half-dome
of light and a busy trunk bumping with each rut
in the road and the bass from Fleetwood Mac's
"Rhiannon." *Which rockstar inside the cab picked*
that *one*, I wonder, mangling the words. We sway
and when the sky is starless, shriek, *taken by*
taken by the sky. Turning off the highway, my friend
tumbles into me. *Dreams unwind.* The car behind us
speeds onward. Maybe we weren't going *that* fast.
Street lights flicker like fireflies. *Love's a state of mind.*

Above the Goat Farm, Half Moon Bay, California

Ira Batra Garde

On a whim, we've set a kite above the goat farm.
Coastal winds motivate her gusting and begging, while

we encourage her, with firm pulls, to take flight. Magenta,
green,
pink ribbons—like long tendrils fluttering—animate her
octopine form.

With our eyes wide, we look up at her wide-eyed, half-moon
face.
Resilient, bobbing, she recovers height with each tug upon the
taut string.

Her effort's insistent. There's persistence visible.
Once she's aloft, we tell ourselves we can do anything

if we can do this. We even believe
we must be good parents if we can teach this—

harnessing the wind for joy

Butterfly Effect

V. P. Loggins

after Larkin

Would the world have been different
If Icarus had flown toward the moon
Instead of the sun? Was his downfall
Fully his fault? Consider: what if
His father, Daedalus, had advised a
Nighttime escape? Of course, the boy
Refused to heed the advice of his father
Regarding the heat of the sun, but had
The two of them decided to fly

Out of their prison at night, and had
Icarus succeeded in his attempt, escaping
With his dad, his wings fluttering like
A butterfly's before the moon, perhaps
In gratitude and relief he may have helped
To turn the world into a garden of tolerance
And forgiveness where fathers would ask
No more of their children than to be wholly
Who time will show them to be. The world

Of pressures inflicted by one generation
Upon another, by fathers, for instance, upon
Their sons, either knowingly or unknowingly,
Would by Icarus's flight in the silver light
Of the moon have awakened a parent's eyes
To a child's struggles and not so much
To his failures. He wouldn't have become
A symbol of hubris and its constant brother
Instability, but of the stabilizing virtue of

Humility. By soaring so close to the brightest
Of lights in the night sky and haloed by
That light Icarus may have been ordained
To teach the world how to love completely,
And no one by such teaching would ask
No more of others than to accept the notion
That love is a nightly mystery conveyed
Like soft moonlight. Had Icarus, dear boy,
Flown near the moon, perhaps Narcissus

Would not have fallen for the watery image
And lived to be a kind old man. Perhaps
Icarus, too, would have survived to be ancient
And had a gentle, generous relationship
With his children, and his grandchildren would
Have carried their grandfather's example forward
Until all nations learned to live in kindness with
Their neighbors like the loving light of the moon
Rather than with the cruel grip of a parching sun.

Camp dad

M.E. Mishcon

The day dad left was not really the day he left. No way.
He was gone long before that. Being the kid, hard to say
exactly when he started to dematerialize, but I do recall when
he actually walked out. December 7, 1995. That was a day of
infamy, all right.

Come to think of it, that day at our house did resemble
Pearl Harbor . . . minus the palm trees. Around here,
December, even early on, is all about ice and snow. But like
the day Pearl Harbor was bombed (or, for me, the day Kurt
Cobain offed himself), people tend to remember where they
were when bad news hit. My Grandpa (I call him Papa) told
me he was driving to the butcher when he heard about the
attack on Pearl Harbor. Said he was listening to a Benny
Goodman riff when the announcement came through.
Stopped his car in the middle of Main Street and was rear-
ended by someone who was also shocked by the news.

Me? I was in Angela's finished basement when her little
brother, Nathan, ran down the steps chanting, "Kurt Cobain
shot hisself in the head! Kurt Cobain shot hisself in the head,
Kurt Cobain shot hisself in the head!"

The time with dad I was in the living room. Way ironic.
My English teacher, Mr. Linder, would groove big time on
my getting the meaning. Ironically, I was listening to my

parents when I got it. Definition of Irony? What seems normal, isn't.

For example, it *seemed* like a regular night. Dinner had been lentil loaf, mashed potatoes with the skins mixed in, green beans. Mom and dad were having their peppermint tea, talking in the kitchen. Same old. From the living room it sounded kind of like music. Not Mo-Town, R&B, Rap, Jazz, Classical, Alternative, Metal, New Age, Rock, or even Folk. The *Grup* sound has a low bass and a slow rhythm, but picked up from time to time. Mostly it's there's a lot of words you can't get, like those early R.E.M. songs. Anyway, I was lying on the blue corduroy couch that has, like, been in this house ever since I have ever been. I was reading fucking *Catcher in the Rye* . . . if you want to know the truth, adding to my 10,000-league depth of all that is ironic.

They were talking anniversary, number 15. Actually way longer if you counted the living together part. But the married bit had been going on only ever since me. So, it was time to celebrate, right? A sign. I say that celebrations are cover-ups. The way fucking birthday parties are all, "Hey-don't-want-to-think-about-croaking-so-I'll-party-hardy."

I overheard dad say, "Ivy, I'd really rather not do a bash, okay? I'm not in the mood."

Mom was cool. "No problemo. I'm not much into a big gathering either. Too many parties this time of year. Why don't we go off someplace? Shiva can stay with Nana and Papa."

It got quiet then. Her question just laid there like a dork on Ex. I tiptoed closer, caught a glimpse of myself in the reflection of the glass on the Jimi Hendrix poster. My eyebrows were high, my mouth in an "o" of surprise when dad said, "Where in hell would we go, Ivy?"

Mom shrugged. "I don't know. Ireland? You've always wanted to go there. Or Italy? You said just the other day that you'd like to go back to Italy. Or what about someplace spiritual, Israel, India even?"

"What's with all the 'I' countries?"

Mom laughed even though the ax-sharp edge in dad's tone was hard to miss. He had used that tone on me. Once when he caught me scarfing junk food at Tanners or whenever I simply refused to discuss "the grassy knoll" with him, dad would be there trimming me down with that tone.

"Fine, Will," Mom said. I guess she got sliced by the tone too, knew it. "Forget the 'I' countries. How about something closer to home? How about Woodstock? We could go back to Yazgur's farm for a memory fest."

That's when I heard The Nothing. It made the first silence seem like a concert. It went on like the well at Camp Half Moon. You dropped a rock down into it and no matter how long you waited, there was no splash at the end of the stone's throw.

He found a place to live real quick considering that it can be hard to do that around here. We live in Vermont and that means tourists, vacation rentals, weekenders, and all. Still, dad landed a cabin right on Cake Lake. The beast of irony rearing its ugly head again.

It's called Cake Lake because there's a little round island in the middle of the water that sits way high and looks kind of like a birthday cake. You have to have some imagination about it. Anyway, dad set himself up in the guest house of some "area code's" estate. He packed up the good stereo, vinyls, tapes, CDS, pods, banjo, skis, skates, snowshoes, backpack, tent, canoe, basketball, baseball mitt, and his wild cherry red Mix Master (dad likes to bake when he's got a mind to) into his brand new, vintage, mint, candy apple red Mustang convertible (yeah, he's into red . . . figures).

Should have guessed something was up when he got that car. Then he drove the six miles over to the new place on good old Cake Lake. It was a while before he told me anything about why or even that he *had* left. But right off Mom pulled me into the kitchen, sat me down at our battered oak kitchen table, took my hand.

"Shiva . . . your dad, well . . . he's got some problems. Well, he's . . . moved out. I think he may need, well, some time to . . . to . . . chill. Sort things out."

The whole time she was talking, Mom ran her long fingers over the rough part of my knuckles as if her fingers were matches and mine were the striking pad. I wanted her to stop. I didn't want to hear her telling me this. I wanted to go call Angela, my best friend, whose biggest problem always had something to do with the geometry homework. But I sat there, nodded, said I knew already, that we'd be okay. I said that we were together and screw dad if he couldn't take a joke. Mom smiled but it was a shit-ass smile. Really, I have seen some hysterical crying that looked happier than that smile of Mom's.

Never mind geometry or English. What's with biology anyway? No sooner did I get my period than the hygiene teacher, Mrs. French, was all, "And someday you'll go through menopause." What about guys? They must be mainlining some kick-butt hormonal toxin. No one seems to notice or care. Boys will be boys. Apparently, men will be boys, too. And girls? Well, we are women, hear us roar and all.

The first time dad had me out to his house was two months after he had moved. I mean, he never said good-fucking-bye until he was way gone for, like, a week. Anyway, by the time he invited me, I was past pissed, past hurt, and just all curious.

From the outside his new place didn't look like much. There were a whole lot of snow-covered, rickety steps leading up to a snow-piled deck that looked out onto the snow-covered frozen lake. It was okay in a rustic-run-away-from-home sort of way. Nothing like our slate gray colonial with the forest green shutters, crescent moon cut-outs on the top. Not that Mom stayed to compare domestic arrangements. She dropped me off. Literally. Didn't hardly wait for me to get from the car before she tore ass out of there, dirty snow flying off the treads of the Jeep.

He was on the top step smiling, bold. "Hey, Princess," he said.

I took my time climbing up. The snowy steps were slick with a fine sheen of ice. "Haven't you heard, dad?" I said, holding on to the shaky banister. "There's been a coup d'état. There's a new princess in town."

He held the door for me, lifted his chin toward the lake. "There's my heron. See it fly."

We stood there watching the long pointy thing, its spindly legs hanging while the wings stretched wide, taking it across the lake in seconds. "It's not supposed to even be here this time of year. Supposed to have gone south." He shook his head. "It's a sight to see," he said.

I didn't argue.

Inside, I slipped out of my parka, looked around. The first impression I had of dad's new place was of the color brown. The bare wooden floors, the long upright bench that stood for a couch, the threadbare, tweedy armchair that served as his throne in this monochromatic kingdom. It was brown as dirt in there not counting his bright red Mix Master on a counter, a green folded-up ping pong table in the corner, and (can't believe this one!) a brand new pinball machine against the wall.

Pigfucker.

That was the little nickname that I had come up with for dad. Not sure why, exactly. Don't think he was actually doing it with swine. Just didn't put it beneath him as a possibility. Looking at him standing there in Brown Town, arms crossed, narrow faced, bad toothy grin, nearly bald for fuck's sake, he was all, "Welcome-to-my-world." It reminded me of when Angela's little brother, Nathan, was just two and had finally crapped in the toilet and called us all in to take a look at it.

I just stood there as dad moved over to the area of the room that was assigned to act as kitchen. There was a mini fridge, the kind that hotel rooms have stocked with stuff like macadamia nuts, tiny bottles of vodka and scotch. Only when he bent over to open it, I could see a quart of milk, a half gallon of apple cider, and a half dozen eggs just as if he were a real person. It wasn't just the fridge that was small, either. Everything in the place looked shrunken, as if dad had taken to living in a playhouse, the kind boys built up in a tree and didn't allow girls into. There was a tiny sink, a tiny stove with two burners on top. There was a small cast iron pot filled with chili, stew, soup, something brown to match the decor. He went over to it, stirred. Have to say, it smelled okay.

Truth is, dad can cook. Bakes too. Big gooey, iced stuff in combinations no one in their right mind would dream of, and for good reason. Last year, first thing in the morning he appeared at my bedroom door and held out a bright orange, three-layer job, candles blazing. Even had a slice with my juice because dad was big on birthday cake for breakfast. Thing is, I almost ralphed. The cake part alternated lemon, maple, and lime with that super sweet orange icing found on those reject kid cupcakes. The cake *looked* great and all. Texture, moist, firm. It was, like all dad's creations, a fucking commercial for Betty Crocker. But it didn't taste good, go together, work. Thing is, dad made the sort of cake that should appear in a glossy photograph, not on your plate. Especially at breakfast. It was always such a letdown.

Turned out the stuff on the stove was beef barley soup. He served it up in mismatched ceramic bowls and poured apple cider into jelly glasses, put an uncut loaf of brown bread on the cutting board/dining table. Shit. He was making some sort of "Hey-I'm-a-midlife-crisis-monk" point here. As if. If only. There was also a pile of empty wine bottles next to the sink. I had no idea what dad was doing when he wasn't ladling out brown food in his brown room, but the sight of those bottles, still pink from red wine, told me it wasn't all about earth tones. I stuck my spoon in the bowl, slurped. Thin, but flavory. Well, I said he could cook.

"Soup okay?" he asked leaning toward me.

I shrugged. He was not getting me that easy. "Fine, I guess. Salty."

"Too salty?"

I pursed my lips. It struck me through that he cared what I thought. "No. Not too. I've got low blood pressure."

He dropped his spoon into the bowl and laughed, shook his head. His eyes got all squinty and, in that moment, he looked just like him. For a second I felt the way I used to, which was not exactly happy or anything Nick at Night like that. But I used to feel like me. Which meant that things had a certain smell in my nose, taste in my mouth, feel in my hand. After dad left it was like the rules of the universe had changed. Even the law of gravity was up for grabs.

Maybe the soup wasn't salty or the room too brown. Being the new me meant that I didn't know what I thought or felt because nothing I had believed before had turned out to be true after all. I was in a strange country having to be fluent in a language I didn't know squat about. And I was there with dad as my guide. Look where following him had gotten me so far.

"So," I said, "do you have a girlfriend or what?" It was my turn to lean forward, smile.

He stopped laughing abruptly. His face froze the way the on-screen picture does when the satellite dish goes out. The image stops in frame, goes modular, disintegrates into abstract blocks of color, and crumbles like a fallen mosaic before turning black.

He looked down at his shoes, sighed big, looked back up at me. "No, Shiva, I don't have a girlfriend. That's not what this is all about."

"Well, I'm listening, dad. In fact, I'm all ears, except for my mouth," I said, sticking the soup spoon into my maw and waiting. And it was okay waiting. My heart was doing the Pete Townsend thing on that live cut of "Tommy." Charged, ready.

He nodded, sat backwards, let the chair tip back in that way that Mom wouldn't let us do at home. "It's hard to explain, Shiva."

"I'll bet." I took the spoon out of my mouth, tapped it on the table.

He nodded and the chair fell forward with a clack. "Your mother and I . . . well, we've been together, like, forever. Since we were kids. Not much older than you are now."

"Really? Star-crossed lovers at 15? And here I thought our last name was Crane, not Hatfield, McCoy, Capulet, or Montague."

At that instant, I didn't care that he had left us as much as I couldn't stand that his reasoning was so unoriginal. It was one thing to abandon us, another to be a total cliché.

No, that's a lie. I could take the cliché if he hadn't left. Or if he'd come back. Guess I was like him, after all. I was a cliché, too.

He smiled, pulled at his chin. "You're so smart. Really. I'm so proud of you even when you're fresh like that because I can hear how smart you are. But, smart as you are, haven't you ever wondered why your Mom and I didn't have but one child?"

I shrugged, didn't feel like answering. Of course I wondered. I bet every only child on the planet wonders that. I bet every orphan wonders why the parents split. For that matter, I bet every kid with brothers and sisters looks at the mob around them sometimes and thinks better of the situation and all. So it wasn't a fair question. But then, it wasn't a fair situation. And, anyway, I was well past the age when I expected fair in the course of world events. I mean, just look at Pearl Harbor, JFK, Vietnam, John Lennon, Kurt Cobain, not to mention that movies cost nearly eight bucks now. Fair. To paraphrase Tina Turner, "What's fair got to do with it?"

"I've thought about it. Guess I just figured that I was enough for both of you."

He nodded again. "You were. You are. But see, Shiv, when Mom got pregnant . . ."

I got his implication and it so sucked. It was as if he was taking the wrong end of a really big pencil and erasing me, brushing off the pink rubber bits, blowing me away. Fuck that. I was no mistake. I shook my head.

"You were there, dad. You *both* got pregnant. We all did. Don't you get it? Otherwise I wouldn't be here and, guess what? I want to be." As soon as I said it, I knew it was true and felt real calm, the way you might just before the boat you are on is about to sink.

But he leaned back in his seat, started musing and all. "Sure, but I was young. I never got . . . I never had . . . a chance. My shot. I've been going through the motions, don't you see? I've been doing the right thing all along. Acting as if, putting on a good face, you know, pretending."

I stood up, walked over to him. "Could have fooled me."

I pushed him ever so slightly. His chair tilted back, balanced for a second, and then fell heavily to the floor with a loud thwack. He lay there, the wind knocked out of him, blinking up at me. But he was all right. He'd live.

I grabbed my jacket to go. But before I stepped out the door, I caught that the look on his face was way familiar. Yeah, there was a family resemblance, all right. He looked just like me on that day of infamy.

The snow blew around on the deck. I pulled the zipper to my ski jacket up to my chin, looked out at the lake. That heron had taken off again, headed for Cake Island. I watched as its long legs unfolded like landing gear, saw it dip its head into the unfrozen section near the edge, come back up with a fish as green as a gummy bear. It swallowed the fish in one slurp, then took off again. Okay, so dad was right about one thing. It was a sight to see.

Then I trudged down the slippery steps and set off to walk the six miles back home.

Jeez, Dad

Ron Yates

The little Massey Ferguson was considered vintage now, but it had been only a few years old when he purchased it. He'd maintained it since then, at least mechanically, but not so much cosmetically. The old girl—he'd named her Betty Lou after his mother—was showing her age. She could still pull, though, especially in the lowest gear. Pulling power would be needed today as Pete had set himself to the task of extracting stumps from his son's recently acquired property.

Getting the tractor to the jobsite was an ordeal in itself. He hadn't used the trailer in . . . how long had it been? Three or four years, he guessed. He knew the wheel bearings should be greased, a messy and time-consuming job. Pete decided the bearings could wait as he prayed he wouldn't end up like those poor folks he occasionally saw broken down on the side of Highway 431 with a trailer whose axle had collapsed because of a seized bearing. He worried about the tires too and their dry-rotted sidewalls. Oh well, he thought, let's get it hooked up, then drive Betty Lou up the ramps and strap her down. "Please, Lord, help us get there safely," he muttered under his breath.

His son's "mini farm" was 12 miles away, toward the interstate. Pete had signed the note with Tyler, who had not yet established any credit, allowing the young man to purchase a first home for himself and to get out from under the pitiless cycle of throwing money away on rent. "Might as well be flushing hundred-dollar bills down the toilet," Pete had told him. "Never get anywhere like that. When you own it, it's yours. Can't be taken away, and the value goes up over time. It's an investment, but also a responsibility. You think you're up to it?" Tyler had answered, "Hell, yes! I got this."

The old farmhouse needed repair, and parts of the property were overgrown, but there was potential there that gave Tyler purpose, keeping him busy making improvements instead of wasting time on video games and a host of other distractions that could eat away at a young man's life, even his soul. Pete knew from his own experiences how easy it was for impulses to take control and how hard it could be to get back on track once the wheels ran off. He hoped that his efforts at the property—getting those stumps pulled—would serve as encouragement for his son, who had just turned 27, as well as a surprise birthday gift.

He imagined Tyler's grinning appreciation of those ugly stumps being gone. And he remembered a phone call a few days ago from Tyler's sister, Allison—something about having dinner out tonight. Opportunities for spending time with both of his now-grown kids were rare. Anxiety ebbed as he visualized the possibilities.

With the trailer hitched to the truck and the tractor strapped down, Pete was ready to roll, but there was one more detail before he headed out: his companion, Brown Dog. Pete had let him out early that morning as usual, to allow the old fellow to get some exercise. The big German shepherd mix was loved by their handful of widely scattered neighbors, and he enjoyed making his rounds along the dirt roads and through the woods to visit and have his head patted by friends. Some of them occasionally offered a crunchy biscuit, chewy treat, or pork chop bone saved just for him. Now, though, it was time to go, and Brown Dog was taking longer than usual to come back home.

Pete cleared his throat, took a deep breath, and cupped his hands around his mouth. With head back he called with a voice strong for his years: "Oh, Brown Dog . . . come on home, Brown Dog! Wooeee, Brown Dog!" Then he walked around to examine the hitch, tires, and straps one more time.

He added air to one of the tractor tires and connected the trailer lights. Then, as expected, he heard the familiar jingle of Brown Dog's rabies tag against his collar buckle. He was trotting along his familiar wooded trail, crunching through the late October leaves, then up the driveway to sniff Pete's pant legs and to look up expectantly. There was a smile playing about his grizzled muzzle and a sparkle in his eyes as Pete patted his head and rubbed his ears. "Good boy. You just a good ol' Brown Dog. We'll get you a treat later, when we get to Tyler's place." Then he walked around to the passenger side of his faded F-150 and opened the door. "Come on, buddy. Hop in. Time to go."

Brown Dog loved to ride and made a good passenger, sitting up on the tattered seat like a person. He slobbered more than most human companions, though, dripping onto the upholstery or sometimes the dashboard when an interesting sight ahead prompted him to lean forward. Pete often conducted one-sided conversations with him, but this morning his mind turned inward during the 20-minute trip, and he thought about his life: the hardships, mistakes, missed opportunities, good times and bad, along with the narrow escapes.

For years he'd been trying to sweep his Vietnam memories into a partitioned-off area of his mind, a locked box. Holding down a job and functioning as a father and husband had required full immersion in the present, so he shook off those memories—or tried to—like the mud that had clung to his combat boots years before. There'd been a blurred time after Nam that continued for too long, a period when nothing much mattered. Afterward, when Pete was struggling with newly acquired responsibilities, nights had been the hardest. Sleep required unbuckling from quotidian concerns and dropping into an empty space where, unfortunately, the peace was regularly disrupted with the staccato popping of gunfire, along with the buzzing, pulsating drone of insects, birds, and helicopter blades beating against the dense jungle air.

Pete had often been assigned point duty during the last months of his tour. The lieutenant had noticed his ability to focus and his skills at map reading. Pete, determined to make it home, didn't clown around as much as the other men. He regarded each breeze-fluttered leaf, broken twig, creeping insect or reptile, and suspicious spot in the jungle floor that may be hiding punji sticks or other booby traps. He dissected the wall of surrounding sound with the keen ear of an orchestra conductor, listening for the incongruous chirps of an unseen enemy.

There were lots of ways to die in the jungle, and on those nights before he was to pull point, Pete would lie in his tent trying to recall the pre-deployment training reels replete with lessons on snake identification, poisonous plants, predator cats and bears, along with instructions regarding enemy tactics and weapon handling. Now, more than 50 years later, voices and images from the old films, along with personal experiences, still intruded into his dreams. In some of the jungle dreams Tyler was one of the men in his unit, and he was always somewhere he shouldn't be.

In reality Tyler as a child had needed more supervision than he got. Pete and his wife Jill had been committed parents, but the unforeseen problems of raising two kids took their toll. Neither Pete nor Jill was equipped, even though they were both older than the parents of their kids' classmates. Like being back in the jungle, Pete had thought: booby traps everywhere, especially during those preteen years. At 13 Allison, previously sweet and cooperative, veered into uncharted territory, dragging Mom and Dad along with her. As a result Tyler, three years younger and adept at fading into the background, received little parental guidance.

In fact, Pete, thinking all was well with his youngest, was surprised when he got the call from a serious-sounding young man: "Hello, is this Mr. Stillman?"

"Yes. This is Pete Stillman."

"You're Tyler's father, correct?"

"I am. Is there a problem?"

"I'm Brian Queller, assistant principal at Midway Elementary. And yes, we are having problems with Tyler."

Seconds passed. "Well . . . I'm sorry to hear that. What kind of problems?"

"He's giving Ms. Densmore fits. Making vulgar sounds, talking out, arguing back, crawling around on the floor, cursing in class, picking on other students—the ones who are trying to learn. You name it. She's sent him to the office seven times this semester, and I've placed him in ISS on two different occasions, for three days each time. We're running out of options. I'm afraid the next step will be alternative school."

"*ISS* . . . that's in-school suspension, right? Why am I just now hearing about all this?"

"Ms. Densmore has tried calling this number several times as well as Mrs. Stillman's cellphone and work number. Your contact info should be updated if your numbers have changed."

"My wife's at the Bellwether Bank now, downtown. And I've changed jobs too. I work second shift at the Hathaway Millworks warehouse. Getting ready to go in now."

"I see. Give me a second. Writing this down. What about cellphones—"

"I don't have one. My wife changed and took a new number. I got it here somewhere."

"I see. When you find it, please share it with us. Just give it to the secretary and we'll update our records. But in the meantime, we have this problem. I recommend a conference . . ."

The memories of that conversation and the many subsequent conferences circulated through Pete's mind as he steered his truck and the heavily loaded trailer toward his son's property. Getting the boy through school had been a frustrating time of readjustment and lowering of expectations, but somehow— magically it seemed—they had come out the other side. Now Pete was proud of Tyler, his newfound sense of responsibility.

There were also memories of Allison. He'd delighted in her when they were an intact family. He still loved her, of course, even though he didn't see her much. Without his permission images, words, and sounds coalesced in his mind of their last argument, just before she moved out with her mother. Allison was 14 at the time.

Jill had sided with her there at the dinner table: "Why shouldn't she get her belly button pierced? She's becoming a young woman, and many of her friends have done it. She's old enough to choose her own—"

"But *why*?" Pete asked, his voice taking on an edge. "Why does she want to highlight—*show off*—a part of her body that generally stays covered, a part that involves skin and . . . directs attention to other parts." Turning to Allison he continued: "Who are you trying to look sexy for? I don't like the idea of boys looking at you and having those thoughts. Seems kinda slutty—"

"Oh my God!" Allison blurted out as she stood, almost knocking over her chair. She slammed the table, rattling dishes. "Dad. You're just *so* old. You don't understand anything! I can't believe you just called me slutty!" Then she stormed out of the room in a cloud of indignation.

Before he could answer, Jill said, "Nice work. Now you've alienated her even further, and me too for that matter. She's right, you know. You don't understand teenage girls or women or what is or isn't sexy." She stood, wiped her mouth, tossed her napkin. "You do the dishes tonight. I'm going to be with my daughter." Pete sat there—rubbing his head and trying to make sense of what had just happened—before carrying the dishes to the sink.

The warmth of the noonday sun and remembering how things had worked out—in spite of Tyler's behavior problems, an unfaithful wife, and a rebellious daughter—lightened his mood. Things do work out, he told himself, eventually. Navigating his mind through the past and his rig along the highway, he remained alert to every sound while continually checking the mirrors. The light traffic and blue sky contributed to the optimistic atmosphere, loosening the grip of anxiety over bad memories, dry-rotted tires, frayed straps, and possibly dry wheel bearings. Pete reached over and scratched Brown Dog between his ears.

His old friend was riding easily, sitting up and looking straight ahead. Years before he'd been a stray who wandered up when Tyler was 13, after his mother had run off with her banker boyfriend, leaving the boy and his dad to themselves in their modest rural home. Father and son alike welcomed this new addition to the family, a rambunctious, thick-coated rascal who was developmentally about the same age as Tyler. The three of them played and wrestled together, developing a strong bond.

Father and son did their due diligence in trying to find the dog's owner. Whoever it was had given Brown Dog preliminary instruction in shaking hands, and he never lost the urge to extend a paw toward his humans. Now, inside the truck as Pete drove, stewing in his memories, the old dog reached out tentatively. This was a cue for Pete to reach back and rub the paw, foreleg, or behind the ears. Sometimes, though, the paw in its reaching was too heavy, and his claws usually needed trimming. As a result, Pete had grown wary of this loving gesture, having had the thin skin of his forearm ripped and bruised by Brown Dog's big, unclipped paw.

"Okay, buddy, that's enough," he said. "I'm trying to drive and you're giving me old man bruises with that big paw of yours." Then he moved his right hand to the top of the steering wheel, making his tender skin an uncomfortable reach for Brown Dog, who turned back to his window gazing. They maintained this arrangement until they reached their destination: Tyler's property, where there was work to be done.

Truck and trailer parked, Pete hopped down from the cab and immediately regretted the move. The time spent sitting on the sagging seat had aggravated his sciatica, sending a shock throughout his lower back and left leg. "Damn," he muttered through clenched teeth as he leaned against the truck. He waited for the pain to subside; then, as he tried to straighten up, he made a mental note to go see that chiropractor again.

He usually got relief after two or three visits, and the stretches and exercises also helped, if he remembered to do them. He hadn't been doing them, he admitted to himself. I've been busy, he thought. Don't have time for getting down on the floor, pulling up my knees, twisting around. But I should—I *gotta*—start back on those stretches.

In truth Pete hadn't been that busy. Since retirement he'd been doing enough each day to produce a sense of accomplishment—cleaning out gutters, replacing fixtures in the bathroom, a little yard work, vehicle maintenance, and helping Tyler with various projects at his new property. The actual work hours of most days, though, were short. The evenings were spent keeping up with the news, reading, and watching old movies from his DVD collection. He couldn't get reliable internet service where he lived. He had tried for a while, before Tyler moved out, but he didn't enjoy many of the streaming platforms' offerings, even when they played without continual buffering. His DVDs always worked, and he knew what he liked.

Standing crookedly beside his truck—the chiropractor had said he was *antalgic*—Pete looked around the property, reflecting on all that needed to be done. Brown Dog had hopped down after him and was sitting on his haunches, watching. After a moment he raised himself, stepped closer, and licked his companion's hand.

"Good ol' fella," Pete said, rubbing the dog's head. "I believe I mentioned something about a treat earlier. Let's go inside and see what we can find."

During Brown Dog's visits to Tyler's place, Pete let him stay in the house while he busied himself with splitting firewood, caulking windows, or whatever that day's project entailed. Brown Dog was unfamiliar with this new neighborhood, and Pete worried he would wander off and get into trouble. He and Tyler both made sure there was always a bag of their old buddy's favorite crunchy biscuits in the house for whenever he visited.

Pete slapped twice against his blue-jeaned thigh and clucked his tongue. "Come on, boy." Brown Dog pricked up his hears and trotted past Pete toward the porch steps with young-dog energy. Once there he looked back at his companion, limping crookedly toward him, giving in to the pain in his back and hip. Pete remained hopeful that after stretching and moving around, he'd be able to get those stumps pulled. After all, Betty Lou would be doing most of the work.

The movement involved in unbuckling straps, attaching the ramps, and backing Betty Lou off the trailer initially helped to limber up that hip. After easing down from the tractor seat, Pete straightened himself and looked up at the clear autumn sky. The sun's radiant energy was warming the ground, rocks, truck, tractor, and all other objects that, in turn, transferred heat into the air, creating currents. The warmth was an encouraging hand on his shoulders. He rocked his hips a little from side to side then tried to touch his toes. Nope, not yet, but he did make it partway before the pain stopped him. That's okay, he thought. It's getting better. He lifted the heavy log chain from the back of the pickup and attached one end to Betty Lou's drawbar. He coiled the remainder of it—nearly 20 feet—between the seat and fender.

The first stump was that of a small pine they had cut earlier, about eight inches in diameter. Pete hooked the chain around it and climbed back onto the tractor. With all the getting up and down, pressing and releasing the clutch pedal, and bending over, the sciatica was reasserting itself. He needed to press the clutch in order to engage the lowest gear. He managed to do so but not without pain. His chiropractor sometimes asked him to rate his pain from one to ten. This was about a six, Pete thought. He worked the levers, selecting the gear ratio that applied the largest multiplier to the torque of Betty Lou's engine, purring at just above idle.

Lifting his foot off the clutch brought pain again, a level four or five. The forward lurch was gentle with the gearing and throttle set as they were, and the tractor eased forward like a tortoise. Pete looked back to watch the slack disappear from the chain. It rose from the ground, making a taut line from drawbar to stump as Betty Lou continued her ponderous forward progress. He watched anxiously. Then his unease gave way to delight as the stump moved without much resistance, not even enough to coax a deeper exhaust note from the engine. It was abruptly extracted along with its roots, ripping up a grass-covered layer of black earth.

Pleased, Pete faced forward and steered the tractor toward a gully on the back side of the property where the stump would be left to rot. He could have shifted to a higher gear and moved faster, but he wasn't in any hurry. Under a radiant dome of blue, he was comfortable in his recent victory. The rumbling purr of Betty Lou's engine added to his contentment.

As it was being dragged across an expanse of green that had once been part of a pasture, the stump and its root ball pulled up clumps of grass, making a black gash in the earth. Pete was satisfied in the knowledge that soon the culprit would be deposited in its final resting place. As he approached the gully at a snail's pace, he plotted a path that would position the stump as near as possible to the edge. Then, with a little help, gravity would do the rest.

Before dismounting he backed the tractor up to put slack in the chain. He unhooked it. Then, with muscle power, he managed to roll stump and roots a few feet to where the slope became precipitous. Gravity took over then, and the stump bounced downward before settling itself on the rocks and soft dirt of the dry creek bed.

He was satisfied, but straightening up after straining at the root ball produced pain in his hip and numbness in his leg. Attaining a full standing position took several seconds. He tried stretching a little as he regarded the chain lying there in the grass, one end still attached to the tractor. Dreading the thought of lifting and stacking the heavy links beside the tractor seat, Pete decided to let Betty Lou drag it back to the scrubby patch that would soon be incorporated into Tyler's backyard. Only four more stumps to pull.

Pete liked to dispatch the more difficult aspects of a project early on. He considered which stump would be next in line for the chain and Betty Lou's pulling power. The toughest prospect would likely be the remains of a red oak they'd cut down because it was showing signs of blight: trunk cracks and mushrooms at its base. He figured it might put up a fight, but after the ease with which the pine was extracted, he was confident that this stump would also succumb.

Dismounting, hooking the chain, and climbing back onto the tractor produced sharp jabs in his hip, but the most painful part was pressing the clutch pedal. "Damn," he muttered to himself. He considered knocking off early and finishing the job when he felt better, but he convinced himself to continue: This one's hooked up. Let's yank it and see how we feel. Need to make a good show today after all this trouble. What's a little pain to a man?

He straightened himself on the seat, but the burning sensation in his hip and the numbness running down his leg did not relent. He grimaced as he lifted his foot from the pedal. There wasn't much slack in the chain, so the result of applied force was quickly apparent. Betty Lou began to roll forward; then progress stopped. The exhaust note deepened, then rose as the mechanical governor opened the throttle to compensate for the load. Pete turned as far as he could to watch the stump break loose. To his dismay it remained steadfast. Then a new sensation: Something was tilting. Was it the earth? No! Upon facing forward Pete realized the tractor's front end was rising up, wheels already off the ground.

Oh shit! He instantly understood the mechanics of the situation. The engine would not stall in the lowest gear. If he were on sand or gravel, the back tires would slip, but the deep rubber lugs bit firmly into the loamy soil. The engine's torque demanded that something move. Either the wheels had to turn, the stump had to yield, or the tractor would climb its own gearing with the front end rising higher with every revolution of the crankshaft. He must immediately disengage the engine from the driveline. That's what the clutch was for.

But lifting his numb leg against the pain in his hip took too long. Then his foot slipped. Betty Lou's front end continued to rise as gravity pulled Pete backward on the seat. He tightened his grip, astonished at how easily the steering wheel moved from side to side with the tires in the air. Thoughts flashed, providing glimpses into the impending disaster. Within seconds she'd flip over on top of him. Slim were his odds of jumping off to the side. Even if he made it, Betty Lou wouldn't stop until she went end over end, smashing herself to pieces.

He struggled to lift his leg. This time he couldn't miss or let his foot slip. Sensing contact with the pedal, he pressed hard, contorting his backside on the seat against the orange-flashing pain. Then something he'd not considered: the instantaneous falling and abrupt, hard landing. His upper torso snapped forward, slamming his sternum and forearms against the steering wheel. He managed to kill the engine. Then everything was still and quiet.

He trembled there on the tractor, numb in parts of his body. As the adrenaline storm slackened, pain rallied to mount a full assault. He closed his eyes and screamed. A barrage of curse words followed—his entire repertoire. Then he blurted them again. He exhaled, spat blood from his bitten lip, and gingerly lifted each arm. They still worked, but his hip, lower back, chest, and leg throbbed maliciously. Stepping down from the tractor unleashed an army of demons with hot needles, piercing him throughout his trunk and limbs.

He stood shakily, taking inventory. Thankfully, he could walk, albeit with a stumbling lurch as he gave in to the pain. Slowly he covered the fifty or so yards to the house. Slowly he mounted the porch steps. Meeting him at the door, Brown Dog sensed something was wrong. He whined and licked Pete's hand. The door opened into the den area where there was an expanse of rug-covered floor.

Using his throbbing arms and a table for support, he eased down onto his knees, hoping he'd be able to get back up. Hand on the floor, he sank onto his right side. From there he turned, propping on his elbows as he slowly settled himself. When he was flat on his back, Brown dog curled up beside him, resting his muzzle against his thigh. Pete reached to rub his friend between the ears. Lying still, his pounding heart incrementally returned to a near normal tempo as the pain relented, providing opportunity to think about what had happened.

A sense of awe overwhelmed him, and he began to pray. "Thank you, Lord, for saving me one more time." His prayer of thanksgiving, with requests for the safety of his children and loved ones, continued silently until he dozed off into a vibrating haze of love. From there Pete dropped into a dream state filled mostly with images of Tyler and Allison during happy times, opening presents, laughing, and playing with their toys.

He had no idea how much time had passed or even where he was when he was awakened by Brown Dog's excited barking. He raised himself painfully, blinking his eyes into focus as the door swung open. A young woman stepped through, pretty and familiar. He blinked again and noticed that Brown Dog was sniffing her and wagging his tail.

Suddenly she pushed ahead, dropping her purse to the floor. "Oh my God! Dad! Are you all right? What happened?"

She knelt beside him.

"Allison," he said. "What are you doing here?"

"Are you hurt? What's wrong? Can you move?"

"Yes, I can move. Just taking a little nap. My back's out of whack."

"What happened? Is it your heart? Something seems really wrong."

"Just got a little twisted up, that's all. I'll be okay. But I wasn't expecting you. Why aren't you at work? And where's your brother?"

"Dad, I called you last week. Today's Tyler's birthday. Remember? I told you I was coming. He's on his way here now."

"Oh, yeah. I knew that."

Allison shook her head, looked at her father with concern etched into her brow. "Come on. Let me help you up. You'll be more comfortable on the sofa."

Rising was awkward. Using his right arm and leg, along with Allison's support on his left side, they made it to the sofa.

Seated there they talked about unremarkable things: her job in Atlanta and her birthday present for Tyler, a Home Depot gift card. He told her about the stump-pulling project, skipping over the details of the accident. She revealed her plans for taking them to dinner, but he would need to shower and change clothes. "I hope you feel up to joining us, Dad," she said, rubbing his calloused hand. "We'll get you a nice steak."

"Not this time, baby. Pretty worn out." Then they heard Tyler's truck in the driveway.

"There he is," Allison said. "Are you sure you're okay? I think you should see a doctor. I mean, can you even walk?"

"I can walk." Then he proved it by standing and taking a few steps toward the door as Tyler was coming in. "Happy birthday, Son."

Tyler clasped his father's shoulders, held him at arm's length. "Hey, Dad, you okay?"

"Yep. When you get settled, come out and help me drop the trailer. Gonna leave it and the tractor here for a few days until I can get back over and finish pulling those stumps."

"You been pulling stumps? Jeez, Dad."

Pete shuffled out onto the back porch with Brown Dog beside him. Moving toward the steps, he heard his children greeting each other and the concern in their voices.

Gripping the handrail, Pete said to Brown Dog, "Easy, buddy. Don't knock me down." Then the two of them made their way toward the truck and trailer. Twilight was approaching. With the sun poised just above the horizon, Pete was glad for the light that remained.

Recalcitrant Spirit
Kimberly Clair

I gave my stepdaughter a book I wanted. I figured I'd find it after she returned to college, stuck between her sheets or buried in the laundry basket. Instead, I found it in the bathroom, splayed over the top of the trash can, the pages damp from a recent shower. Lucy hadn't left yet. Her orange car was still parked in the driveway, blocking us in. A crusty bong sat on her desk. She'd always arrive with so much stuff, it took multiple trips, from car to bedroom, to get it all inside. An oblong pillow with cherubs embroidered on one side, an oil lamp that fell to pieces in my hands. I had no idea where she'd gotten these things or why, for the two short weeks of her winter break, she couldn't bear to live without them, but these weren't the right questions for the stairs, the ritual schlepping of mysterious items. As soon as the pillow and lamp had found their rightful place in her room, she'd be gone again, visiting high school friends, getting a new tattoo, checking in on her mother. There was only so much one could learn lugging a wicker basket full of wigs.

The book I'd given her for Christmas was by a contemporary essayist on the topic of love. I'd heard good things about it. I read the introduction and got partway through the first chapter before I realized I wasn't one of those people who could read on the toilet. All I could think about was how cold and vulnerable it was down there. By the time I finished washing my hands, love had flittered away, like a hummingbird you never really saw to begin with.

We only had them on the weekends—Lucy and her older sister, Caroline—and I used to put considerable effort into planning activities we could all do. Hikes, homemade movies, trips to the beach—all part of my plan to get them to like me. By late middle school, they had their own plans and activities, but it still came as a shock, after Lucy left for college, how empty and bare our weekends had become.

My husband started running marathons. Dan had always been a runner, but he had nothing to show for it, by which he meant medals. He signed up for 10Ks and half marathons and charity races and soon had an assortment of silver and gold discs draped over the laundry closet.

I took up meditation. I found a free guidebook from a Hindu temple down the street and set up in Caroline's bedroom, which faced east. This was the correct direction to face when meditating, according to the guidebook. Also, it was important to choose a room that had neutral consciousness—ideally not an office or a bedroom. I didn't know if Caroline's room counted as "neutral," but she hadn't lived there for five years, so I figured whatever consciousness had been residing there had had plenty of time to even out.

I bought a meditation cushion and constructed a small altar by the window, where Caroline had left an onyx Dalmatian statue standing guard. I gathered that my meditation practice was supposed to be a solitary endeavor, but I liked the idea of having company, at least in the beginning. The guidebook had failed to mention how incredibly boring it was to just sit there with all your thoughts. Although, I guess the point was to not pay attention to your thoughts. Or was it to focus so intensely on your thoughts that they stopped becoming important or noticeable at all? Every time I did the laundry, my husband's rapidly expanding collection of medals clanged contemptuously.

If my efforts were consistent and sincere, the guidebook promised, I would start to see results. It didn't say what those results were, exactly, but after several months, I noticed a slight reduction in my overall resistance to the practice. It no longer felt strange and pointless to be sitting there alone in Caroline's bedroom while my husband added another medal to his collection. It felt nice. Peaceful.

But there was something else. Something secret, indescribable. About six months in, I became aware of a mysterious presence in the room with me. Not a ghost, exactly. Nothing ominous. Just a gentle, subtle force that came to me only after I had freed my mind from all distractions and calmed my heart to the point where it may not have been beating at all. In that state, I had no awareness of time or my body's aches and pains. All of my attention was focused on summoning and sensing that presence.

What was it? It had a shy, mischievous quality. Almost as soon as I detected it, it would dart away like a squirrel stealing figs. It filled me with a kind of sweet, innocent joy I had never felt before—a joy that was also strangely sad, tinged with longing. And yet, it seemed, this force longed for me, too. The guidebook said nothing about this, but I took my discovery of this mysterious force as a clear sign of progress. I started meditating for longer and longer periods, every morning and evening. It seemed that the more closely I mirrored the qualities of this mysterious force—peaceful, gentle, and still—the more likely it was to visit me. When it did come, I tried to keep it with me for as long as possible.

Meditation began to feel like a game—a child's game, innocent and delicate. I learned to relax my muscles at will and empty my mind of nearly all thoughts but one. *Where are you?* It always came, eventually. I no longer had any difficulty fixing my attention on a single point, as the guidebook had recommended. My attention belonged exclusively to the force, with its irrational, magnetic allure, like a friend pulling you into trouble.

One evening, while my husband was out running with friends, I decided to meditate at sunset. The guidebook said that this was a particularly auspicious time. I lit a candle and performed a few basic yogic poses to help my body relax. I mentally recited a simple prayer the guidebook had suggested, then I exhaled deeply and began to concentrate.

The force came almost immediately. This time, there was nothing subtle about it. It washed over me like a warm wave, somehow enveloping me both from within and without. At once, I became aware of how heavy and burdensome my body was—a giant sack of water struggling to stay upright. And then, the weight of that burden receded and I felt the force take over, holding up every muscle, every cell. Even now, I struggle to describe exactly what was happening to me. All I knew was that this otherworldly presence was smoothing out every jagged corner of my heart, polishing every rusted edge that had existed within me. I understood that this feeling was all I'd ever wanted, was what I'd been craving with every fiber of my being since the moment I was born.

Something crashed behind me. The bedroom door swung open.

"You're *home*?" My husband's cheeks were flushed. "I've been calling you. I forgot my keys!"

I knew I was supposed to say something, but I could barely move. I was still adjusting to idea of having a body.

Dan flicked several leaves off of his jacket and continued to glare at me. "How long have you been in here?"

It felt like a processing problem, as if my brain had just rebooted. A wheel was turning, but few commands were going through. Eventually, I managed a shrug and he left me alone and I tried to understand what had happened. I had gone somewhere, even though I had not gone anywhere. And my husband had climbed through our bathroom window in order to get inside. *That* felt like the dream, and wherever I'd just been felt like reality. The only reality I ever wanted to be in. But now it was gone.

Eventually, I found my phone, which was lying next to the Dalmatian. It was almost 10. I'd been meditating for three hours.

Dan signed up for the Vienna marathon in the spring, and we all went to visit Caroline, who had been living there, studying art, since she graduated from college. During the day, we'd follow her around the city like children, pointing at random statues and plaques, asking for a brief history of everything.

By late afternoon, when our feet were sore and our questions had dried up and my hips were killing me—too much meditating, Dan said—Caroline's boyfriend, Walter, would join us, and a new wave of intrigue would bubble up, fueled in large part by the beer and Aperol spritzes that flowed in a steady stream until well past midnight.

I'd lost all interest in drinking. In most things, actually, since I'd been transported to the other realm. The world—this realm—felt real again, but it had lost its importance, like a piece of jewelry from an ex. We ate Sacher Torte and strolled the grounds of Schönbrunn Palace where Walter worked and gave us a private tour. We sweated uncontrollably in the Schmetterlinghaus while four hundred exotic butterflies drifted over our heads. We watched the slow, measured prancing of horses trained at the Spanish riding school, and I went to my first opera, glancing from stage to screen in the stuffy, upper box. And it was great, it really was. But the force was always somewhere in my mind, tugging at my attention. *Are you here now? When are you coming back?* I couldn't believe I had lived my entire life without ever knowing such a thing could exist.

On the day of the Vienna marathon, we all broke our promise to get up at 5 and accompany Dan to the starting line. By the time I woke up, he had already finished and was making his way back to the hotel.

We celebrated at Caroline's apartment that evening, after Walter got back from work. He'd offered to make us spaetzle, and while he brooded over the stove, Caroline and Lucy took turns manning the turntable—one of two pieces of furniture that populated the living room. The other was a couch, which Dan immediately sank into, medal flopping over his chest.

Caroline had always been the more subdued and pensive sister; Lucy was more goofy and playful. But as they'd gotten older—or maybe it was all the wine?—these sharp distinctions had loosened and fallen away. Meditation had taught me to be "aware" of my thoughts, and as I watched them twirling around the living room, hair flying into each other's faces, I noticed how increasingly fascinated I was by their adultness, how, in such a short period of time, they had evolved into such complete human beings, with their own distinct laughs and hairstyles, each with a whole universe of problems.

Dan's head was drooping even before Caroline brought out dessert. I let him finish his wine, then took his arm and helped him down the steps onto the street where our Uber was waiting.

"You did great, honey," I said, kissing his cheek. "Don't you think?"

He was too tired to respond. He just shrugged and pushed his medal to the other side of his chest like it was a colossal nuisance.

At home, I started waking up at 4:30 so I could meditate for two hours before I had to go to work. In the evenings, while Dan read quietly in bed, I disappeared into Caroline's room for another two to three hours. On the weekends, I fasted and sat for as long as I could, usually around four hours. But the force was hiding from me. I knew it could sense my neediness, my desperation. I was trying too hard, but what else could I do?

"Getting cooked" was a term runners used to refer to overexertion, going so hard that you end up unable to run at all. These days when I meditated, I could barely keep my eyes open, let alone concentrate. My stomach gurgled, my hips burned, my feet fell asleep. The more I ignored my body, willing it into submission, the louder it screamed back, like a toddler I'd shut in a closet, pretending it didn't exist. Desperate, I revisited my guidebook, looking for some key phrase that would help me unlock the portal to that other realm. Instead, a single sentence popped out at me. It was the only sentence in the whole guidebook that was underlined and yet, somehow, I'd never really noticed it. "In meditation," it said, "nothing should be forced."

"You know they don't give medals for meditation," Dan pointed out. I understood that the bitterness in his voice came from having lost his movie night partner, his Saturday morning cappuccino partner, his partner to read with in bed. But I was so bleary and brokenhearted, his bitterness barely penetrated. At last, I decided, he was right. I didn't need to torture myself trying to recreate something from the past. Wasn't the whole point of meditation to be present? To focus only on the now?

I cut back to just a half hour every morning and evening. But the force had other plans for me. It started visiting me outside of my meditation sessions, often during the most mundane moments of my day—sending emails, making a salad. At first, I was thrilled. It was just like that first time, this subtle, gentle vibration sneaking up on me, wanting to be known. It buzzed around my neck while I had meetings, brushed against my shoulders while I ate lunch. I laughed, thinking about how dogged I'd been since we returned from Vienna. Of course it would return to me now that I had relaxed my efforts.

But there was something different about the force. Or maybe it wasn't the same force at all. This force was pushy, insistent. It woke me up in the middle of the night, sliding up and down my spine like a witch's finger, sticking in all my sensitive spots. It zapped between my ears while I showered, prickled my feet while I was trying to rest. I began to experience a feeling of dread whenever it found me. Was this really the same force that had captured my heart and lured me into an ecstatic, timeless trance? Was this just another one of its games?

I didn't tell Dan about these developments. It seemed out of his realm of expertise. Instead, I called the number on the back of my guidebook. On the fifth ring, a woman answered. She seemed to be in the middle of lunch. I told her my predicament.

"Oh dear," she said after sustained chewing. "That's not good, is it?"

"Have you ever heard of anything like this before?" I asked.

"No, no. Nothing like that."

I waited for more—a follow-up, or at least some comforting advice—but none came. The chewing resumed.

"What should I do?" I stammered.

"Let me ask you this," she said, slowly. "Are you sure that you followed the instructions exactly?"

In the fall, I discovered a Zumba studio within walking distance from my house. The walls were bright pink and when the class started, they lit the room with black light, which made our teeth purple in the mirror. The studio could only fit 20 people. It was chaotic and sweaty and loud and I loved it. The amount of effort it took to trace the instructor's movements and replicate them with my own hands, feet, and hips absorbed all of my attention, allowing no other thoughts to filter in, which was exactly what I wanted. The force didn't bother me at Zumba. In fact, after a few weeks of avoiding meditation altogether, it finally left me alone, disappearing into the ether.

One evening when I returned from class, I couldn't find Dan anywhere. His backpack was on the couch in the living room, and his keys were in the dish we kept on the kitchen counter. I went into each of the rooms calling for him and felt a strange tension in the house, perhaps the way animals can sense a storm. On my second trip downstairs, he emerged from the bathroom in the guest room.

His face was blank. "What day is it?" he asked.

"Monday. Are you okay?"

His gaze fell on his computer on the other side of the room. He went to it, opened his email, then turned back to me. "What have I been doing for the past couple of hours?"

I noticed his guitar was propped up against the desk. "Playing music?"

But he didn't hear me. He was scrolling through his emails, his eyes pinched in confusion.

"Who's John Shaefer?" he asked. "Who's . . . Ari Laroche?"

These were the names of his colleagues. I laughed, pretending it was a joke.

"Come on. You know who they are. Did you eat dinner?"

"I don't understand this." He seemed transfixed by the emails. "I don't understand any of this." He turned to me, his expression severe. "Can you tell me what I've been doing for the past couple of hours?"

"I just did," I said. I felt the purr of disquiet in my stomach, the same feeling I had when the force started zapping me during my meetings. "Did you go to work today?"

"I don't know." He dropped into the couch. "I can't remember. What day is it?"

I took his temperature and his pulse—both normal. No signs of paralysis. No slumped gait. I asked again about whether he'd eaten, but he couldn't remember. He wasn't interested in food. He started wandering around the house, peering in each of the rooms as if expecting to find some important clue, something glimmering with recognition. As I followed him, we cycled through the same set of questions. *What day is it? What have I been doing for the last couple of hours? How long have I been like this?* Ten minutes later, the questions would start all over again.

It was unnerving to see my husband like this—a man who had run four marathons in the past year after never having run one in his life. A man who always knew what to do in a crisis, like climbing through the bathroom window after locking himself out of the house. I certainly wouldn't have thought of that. I would've slept in the backyard, covering myself with leaves.

Dementia didn't just happen to a person out of nowhere, I reasoned. It was a gradual decay with telltale signs. The more we wandered around the house, cycling through the same questions, opening the same doors, the more certain I became that this wasn't dementia or some mysterious health condition. It was me. I had done this. If you traced the thread of this moment all the way back to its root, you would find me sitting innocently on my meditation cushion. Me and my unbearable longing

It was close to midnight by the time I convinced him to go to bed. He still didn't know what day it was or what he'd been doing for the past hour, so I offered to tell him a bedtime story, a one-of-a-kind invention, just like I used to do when the girls were young.

"Once upon a time," I said, "there was a frog. A very crotchety, lonely old frog that none of the other frogs liked."

I waited for one of his four questions, but he was quiet.

"This old frog actually had a crush on another frog, a grandmotherly frog who liked to make dresses out of lily pads, but he knew it was a long shot because of his terrible, croaking voice."

My husband closed his eyes.

"It was truly jarring. Whenever he spoke, all the other frogs in the pond hopped as far away from him as they could. This poor old frog didn't know what to do. When he tried to ask for help, his terrible scratchy voice split all the lily pads in half and made the tadpoles cry."

"Honey?" His voice was softer, no longer spiked with panic. "Can we go to sleep now?"

I let out a giant sigh of relief. Not only because I was free from the responsibility of having to finish my idiotic story, but because it was the first new sentence he'd uttered in almost five hours. We were going to be okay.

The tests all came back normal, just as I knew they would: the MRI, the PET scan, the EEG. For that last one, a Russian man in his sixties came directly to the house and slathered Dan's head with jelly before affixing the electrodes. They were penny-sized buttons with a trail of colorful wires that fell to his hip and connected to a battery pack he'd have to wear for 72 hours. I took lots of pictures.

Without medical evidence, Dan's doctor declared the cause of his memory lapse to be "excessive running." Getting cooked. I don't know how convinced Dan was by this hypothesis, but he didn't want to take any chances. He put all of his running gear in a tub and left it in the garage so he wouldn't be tempted.

Suddenly, there was so much time. It got too cold and dark for evening walks. We spent most evenings in front of the fire, watching the flames rise up and fold in on themselves. I kept waiting for him to blame me, to make the connection between my obsessive pursuit of eternal presence and the temporal glitch in his consciousness, but he never did. Eventually, like all things that aren't regularly tended to, my guilt shriveled up and faded away.

"You'll run again," I told him.

He squeezed my hand. "I know."

In December, just before Lucy was scheduled to arrive for Christmas, I found the book I'd given her the year before, the book on love. It was in the backyard on one of the tree stumps that ringed our firepit. The book was mostly ruined from rain, but a small chunk in the middle was still legible. I sat on the stump under the crooked palms and opened to a random page.

The author wrote about a feeling she'd once had, which might have been love, although she wasn't entirely sure. And she couldn't say exactly when she'd had it, or when she'd lost it, only that she knew it was no longer with her. It was only a memory, now, flickering inside her like a spirit, forever dancing between worlds. This thing, she wrote, was the only thing a person ever really wanted, and yet, looking at it head-on, you could never really see it. It wasn't the type of thing that wanted to be seen.

I couldn't read the rest—the ink was too runny—so I closed my eyes and let the book fall out of my hands. I felt my spine instinctively straighten. I relaxed all tension from my muscles, the way I had practiced so many times before. I imagined the weight of my body falling away and let my breath move in and out on its own. If I was still enough, I thought, the force might come back to me. But my focus was off. I couldn't quite go there. I was too busy listening for the sound of Lucy's car pulling into the drive.

CASE 16: Instructions for Extraction
Samantha E. Woodruff

How to Thread a Wound

Dear Sixteen,
Your rib cage is showing, and your spine is
e x p o s e d
so prominent, I could play a sad symphony
with your brittle bones, and it would echo.
Have you counted the calories in Plan B?
You've been eating them
like chalky hearts in February.

I imagine I could reach through a black hole
and come out the other side swinging;
wrap my fist around the precise moment
you stifled your intuition and swallowed
the skeleton key to your own cage.

String theory proposes that eleven dimensions
exist in our universe simultaneously—
and I can't rest knowing that I live harmoniously
while the other ten of us are trapped
and never leave him.

Sixteen, you aren't going to make it
if you auction off your self-worth
one *I'm sorry* at a time,
and shrink yourself to stay
bound to a collapsed star, mistaking him for daylight.

When he threads constellations from your shame—
can you call that love *authentic?*

Listen, Sixteen,
I could traverse every dimension to reach you,
just to rattle your cage until your teeth chatter
and you let that rage seep into your skin.

S e p a r a t e

the soft tissue and corrupt the marrow
deep in your bones.
(*You know.*)

They tell us time is linear, but I disagree.
I circle back to you often.
Some days, I don't know if I want to time travel
and hold you close,
or take you by your throat.

The universe is fond of synchronicity.
In Japan, there is a legend of red thread
that binds us by our pinky fingers.
I know you and I are intertwined;
your "sixth sense" is me,
playing tug-of-war with our lifeline.

I hope the same thread snakes
through the vacant chambers of his heart
and severs them into quarters we can disburse—
trophies for a string of wronged women.

This I promise:
You draw the poison from your wounds
and weave the crimson venom into a tapestry
with the threads of your pain,
while he withers in self-made misery,
a purgatorial record skip
–ing
over the same scratch.

Your bones grow stronger with age,
as you leave behind the warden of your prison
and escape his sentence.
You save your own life and live
to give others their breath.

Yours,
Thirty-Six

abraded

Eleanor Thalheimer

1.

Don't misunderstand the situation. Dana considers herself a bad Jew—confirmed to her childhood synagogue like a Presbyterian instead of properly Bat Mitzvahed (don't ask); she missed High Holy Day services 15 years in a row during her twenties and thirties.

But anyone could mistake her for a good Jew this bright fall Friday in Portland, Oregon. In her small kitchen with teal Marmoleum floors, Dana marries yeast and sugar, cracks eggs, sprinkles salt, and sets challah dough to rise. Later, she punches down the second proof, the yeasty air releasing like a sigh. This ritual is done in relative peace: Her kids are still at school, husband at work, and she met her last graphic design deadline that morning. The crisp air is still, sunlit, and lush with Joni Mitchell's *Blue*. A musky jasmine smell exudes from Dana's body; she's fully and remarkably showered.

Dana will look back on this kind of challah-making several months later and be nostalgic. The simple joy will be joined by unpleasant emotions, like defiance. If you had a chance, you might even taste the change in Dana's delicious challah—the yeast hungrier, the braid tighter, the egg wash thicker, richer, and acorn-brown.

But today she hums with Joni. The heels of her hands mash the elastic dough. It's warm from the fermentation, which will balloon and swell the bread. She folds it in half and mashes, folds, and mashes.

Satisfied her kneading has enthused the gluten, Dana slices through the dough with her kitchen blade. The inside is striated like a tree stump and dotted with fermentation bubbles. Six strands for their Shabbat table and a four-strand round for their neighbor Audrey, who just had a baby. Dana pledged fresh bread (most) every Friday to Audrey during her fourth trimester with baby June.

The strands contract after each roll out. Her hands are more wrinkled and sunspotted than a 45-year-old's should be. That's what a string of summers following Phish will get you. In her closet, she hides the late 1990s photos of herself wearing homespun backless tank tops made of fabric scraps. Dana has no regrets, beyond the ridiculous sandy brown dreadlocks.

Those summers when dirt stained the calluses of her feet, she belonged in a way that she never had before or has again. Dancing with her flowy skirted, slackline-setting, hack-sacking brethren, love came into her through the earth it seemed. All too soon after college, several fell into addiction and many into cubicles. At the same time, she found Rich, a former Marine and security analyst. Despite the fact he was square as hell, she belonged with him.

Her grasp is soft on the cables of dough. As she crosses strand over strand, she senses her great-great-grandmother Ruth's hands. She never met Ruth, but her challah lives on in legend. Those weathered wrinkly hands superimpose her own. Dana knows this.

Challah is love. Over the pandemic, when her family looked at each other every night, stunned by their isolation, the Friday ritual became an anchor to their weeks, which turned into months and years. In the challah, she braided her love, anguish, hope, fear. When she felt nothing but numbness, she still braided, leaning into muscle memory.

Rolling out Audrey and June's challah, she wishes them nourishment.

A quick note about Dana: She found Phish's music a spiritual experience (she would admit this to no one but her husband and her two close friends). Dragging her fingertips over the bark of an old-growth Douglas fir eight miles into the wilderness is also spiritual. For Dana, anything that brings her closer to the mystery of being human is spiritual. She isn't audacious enough to think she could understand, rather she warms herself next to mystery like a fire. She craves proximity.

Gathering for Shabbat is proximity, like swaying to "The Mango Song," the version on her '98 Phish bootleg. To be honest, this surprises Dana.

She brushes the egg wash over Audrey and baby June's challah. Dana doesn't know Audrey very well, but one must take good care of neighbors. The interwoven strands represent community.

Elisa and Brooks burst through the door, backpacks dangling from their arms. The peace pops like a bubble. She goes to them and opens her arms.

2.

"Can I bring it to them?" Brooks stamps his seven-year-old feet, his wild tawny curls quivering.

Dana, Brooks, and Elisa stand on the sidewalk outside of Audrey's small Craftsman house. The Japanese maple out front is already aflame in late September. Dana lifts a paper sack holding warm challah beyond the reach of the children's grasping hands.

"No, me! You did it last time," says Elisa, who is two years older but nonetheless adamant. Her dark eyes flash; she always seeks justice. The tattered bunny perpetually squeezed in her fist dilutes her ferocity.

"I wonder if there's a way for you guys to deliver it together." Dana taps her index finger on her lips. "Hmmm."

They settle on each holding the loaf with one hand, as if they were on either side of a heavy trunk, and walk it to the front door.

At this point, it's important that you know Dana's entire extended family voted for Trump in 2016, except for her closeted cousin Greg, but don't rat him out.

Dana. Could. Not. Believe. Her. Family. Voted. For. Trump.

They're from Shreveport, Louisiana, part of the small Jewish community descended from German potato-farming immigrants. Long story short, the political rift felt too big. She has no relationship with her family anymore. This summary of Dana's estrangement is overly simple, but Dana's pain isn't. She misses her dad.

Her family is a ghost appendage. Still, she can't imagine looking them in the eyes. Her father says blood is thicker than water, that her absence is a betrayal. But to Dana there is right, and there is wrong. Bad guys and good guys.

Dana fashions her own community, loose webs of acquaintances fortified with grocery-store hellos and borrowing shovels. A prosthetic. She also tries to build community with the families from her kids' Jewish day school, where they suddenly and surprisingly switched last year from their increasingly violent neighborhood school. There was incredible fortune in the timing.

But, as established, Dana fancies herself a bad Jew, never going to Saturday services or fasting on Yom Kippur. Dana seems to only fully belong with Rich, Elisa, and Brooks. Oh, how her 23-year-old feminist self would tsk.

Audrey answers the door with baby June strapped to her chest and cheers, which the kids love. Her pixie-cut blonde hair is cowlicked in various places, and dark circles are under her lake-green eyes.

Dana and Audrey, neighborhood-block-party friends, always ask after each other's art when they see each other. It's easy to fall into mom talk—strollers, sickness, school—but Audrey and Dana don't. Audrey writes songs. Dana writes poems. They talk about one day collaborating. It's sustaining to dream.

Audrey takes the round of challah out of the bag. Her fingers are delicate on the golden braid. She touches it to her button nose and inhales for a luxurious amount of seconds. "Thank you," she says. Dana doesn't know this, but Audrey does feel the deep nourishment.

Dana stays at the sidewalk, resisting the urge to peer at the perfect baby, honoring the sacred space of a newborn and her mama. While she might be a bad Jew, she is a good hippie. "Eat bread and keep the faith, my friend."

3.

Later, in early November, Elisa is late for her tumbling class. Dana holds her hand as they scuttle quickly down the sidewalk. The sky is a sooty blanket of thick clouds. They can walk everywhere in their beloved neighborhood.

They hear the protest before they see the sea of people marching down the side street near the tumbling studio. Dana's stomach slinkies. The entrance to the studio will be lousy with protesters. Dana has to decide: Turn back or push through.

"From the River to the Sea, Palestine will be free!" a group of white moms in Lululemon pants chant.

Dana stops short, pulling Elisa to a halt. She takes a deep breath, releases it, and squats to come eye to eye with her beautiful daughter. She wavers about what to say. There are many options.

"We have to walk through these people, honey, and I want you to pay attention. We probably marched with some of them in the Black Lives Matter protest, remember that?"

Elisa is solemn and nods.

"I thought that was good, but sometimes people just follow other people because they like the way it feels, not because they understand a situation. Without nuance, they can become what they think they are fighting. It's tricky. Do you understand?"

"Kinda." Elisa's eyes absorb Dana's face.

How could she? Dana doesn't understand fully.

"Want to make our way through or turn around?"

Elisa grasps Dana's hand. "Through."

Dana stands and walks forward. Elisa clings to her.

Dana pauses. "Oh, no, honey. Chin up, shoulders out. That's how we do this."

Spittle is what Dana most remembers from this protest. As you know, Dana is a graphic designer. She thinks in images; they build her memories.

She remembers the spittle from her neighbors' screaming mouths. Droplets fly through the air. Foam gathers at the creases of the mouths. They wear clogs and Prana pants with Keffiyehs. Patagonia jackets with bandanas and face masks disguising their identities.

Dana and Elisa push through the yelling throng, dodging the wave of Palestine and Hamas flags. People clog the street, so their progress is slow.

Near the studio entrance, Dana's neighbors chant. The moment the words reach her ears will change Dana. From the frothy mouths of *her* people it's tectonic. Her eyes will see differently. Her heart will lean differently. The betrayal will never make sense.

"Resistance is justified if Palestine is occupied!"

Justified: An alum from her children's day school was at the music festival organized in the name of peace. She had ridiculous sandy brown dreadlocks. She was last seen dragged half-naked and bleeding into the back of a pickup truck. The person making the video was very proud. The video was for his mother. He bragged he had already killed 11 Jews.

Dana flings open the entrance door to the tumbling studio, stumbles into the anteroom, and hugs Elisa to her, as if protecting her from an invisible snatcher of children. Her lungs resist filling.

Justified: a baby cut from a living mother's womb.

"I'm going to stay here until the protest passes, so don't worry," Dana tells Elisa, who doesn't let go.

Justified: Raping a grandmother who fights for Palestinian rights. Raping children. Raping women. Raping men.

Two of the tumbling instructors are in the room looking on. Class has already started in the studio. One of the instructors with short hair wears a name tag to remind the children: "Sloan, They/Them." They narrow their eyes on Dana and Elisa.

"Isn't the protest beautiful?" they ask.

"Go on inside, love." Dana unhooks Elisa's arms. "I'll be right here."

Elisa disappears behind the studio doors where children cartwheel.

"No," Dana says to them, stunning herself with the words falling from her mouth. "My family is Jewish, and we don't feel safe. It feels . . . antisemitic."

Sloan cocks their head, as if confused. "Of course there's antisemitism," says the person Hamas would throw off a roof. "Look what Israel is doing."

4.

A month later, Dana and the kids pass Audrey's small Craftsman house. The front door is different, entirely pasted over with a lavender sign. The giant words are in a font that simulates a child's handwriting:

"No Palestinian children deserve to be murdered."

Dana walks faster so her children won't see. She doesn't want them to know quite yet that Audrey doesn't care that Israeli children, Jewish children, were murdered. The sign, which fits a complicated, devastating war into one sentence, tips its hat to an old lie: Jews like to murder children. At first Dana is embarrassed by the cliché of it, before the horror sets in.

"Let's hurry!" Dana pulls them along. "It's going to rain soon." The evergreen-lined sidewalks, raincatchers, free libraries, bioswales, and Love Not Hate signs seem made of Styrofoam.

A message quivers in her DNA. She resists listening but fails. A metallic taste of fear delivers the missive. Dana isn't an expert on history, but anyone could see what's happening, if they cared to open their eyes.

For a second, Dana is disoriented and steers them into a plant boutique, not the coffee shop. For a second, she doesn't know where she is at all.

5.

Crazy stuff happened at multi-day Phish festivals. Some of those stories Dana hasn't even told Rich.

Dana can't keep a specific one out of her head. Before walking through the protest she hadn't thought about it in years. The mental reel plays as she shampoos her hair, listens to podcasts, waits in the school drop-off line. The almost-forgotten story torments her and is alive.

In 1999, a big group of Dana's friends pilgrimaged to the Camp Oswego festival in rural New York. Miles of tents covered the sequestered, sun-pounded county airport.

On the first night at the Camp Oswego festival, the sets were ethereal. Their group of friends danced within a gigantic crowd of half-naked sweating people. Most of them did drugs. But even those that didn't felt high as they stumbled back into the darkness of their campsite after the show.

All the girls but Dana and Clem linked arms for the long trek to the porta-potties. In the darkness, the seven boys drank tepid beers and discussed the night's most wicked parts. Dana and Clem lay in the tent giggling while boys got rowdier outside.

Dana didn't hear the decision being made, but somehow an idea blossomed within the circle of boys; a sudden hush marked a shift in atmosphere. Dana and Clem shushed as well. Around them, people from other campsites talked loudly and laughed; jam boxes competed. Flashlights strobed around. One of their boys lets out a grunt. Both of the girls recognized a furious, fleshy kind of sound. They looked at each other, then rose slowly to the mesh window. The boys didn't realize they were there.

They were shoulder to shoulder, cocks out. Clem's boyfriend was right there. Dana could feel Clem's shock more than see it in the dark.

"Should we break it up?" Dana whispered.

Clem didn't answer, hypnotized. Dana turned back to the outlines of the boys. Their pace quickened, arms moving with a violence. Some threw their heads back, some locked gazes. Others squeezed the shoulder of the boy next to him or bent forward. Moans escaped. The circle strained tighter together; one and another's pleasure drove the momentum, building each other's climax, climbing each other like stairs. Dana felt sucked into the vortex of it, unable to breathe.

You know those gift poppers that older people use at table settings for dinner parties? The ones that have paper tabs that everyone is supposed to pull at the same time, but the pops are never synchronized? That's how the boys came— awkwardly, not at the same time, loud. A thick iron smell filled the air.

"Hurry up, Jordan, before the girls come back." One of them laughed, already kicking dirt over the mess.

She could have sworn that Jordan, who worked in the library and let her stay late in the computer lab, stared at her through the mesh of the tent window as he finished. Ecstatic, shameless, reveling in himself and riding the stares of the others. A froth of spittle gathered at the corners of his mouth. The glut, the betrayal, sent the girls crab-walking across the piles of sleeping bags, quietly out the back door of the tent.

"This never happened," said Clem.

Those seven boys are her Portland. In the past, she has also been this Portland—circled up, clasping the metaphorical shoulder next to her, catching others' eyes, crying out in orgiastic righteousness. Dana imagines Jordan's face is replaced by her own. Clem's shame crawls her skin. Dana has started to wipe flecks of spittle from her own mouth that aren't there. She uses her sleeve or hem, when no one is looking. She can't stop rubbing the delicate creases. They abrade and crack; she still can't stop.

6.

It's spring now, and Dana doesn't give challah to her neighbors anymore, except for Mitzy Blumenthal on 41st, and old man Phil, whose yard is choked with weeds and roof rotting toward collapse. But on this rainbowy late afternoon, she isn't giving challah away; she's having people over.

She lifts the double recipe of dough and whaps it down on the marble countertop. She pounds it, mashes it, folds it. The dough (or is it Ruth?) almost speaks to her when it's ready to be braided. She slices it for six strands, small knots, and rose embellishments—a special bake.

Her phone rings. "What's up? . . . No, that's not necessary . . . just bring yourself . . . yes . . . no, they are excited to see you . . . the only rule is don't talk about politics . . . obviously because your politics are bad . . . Actually! Wait! Can you bring some extra butter? Southern Jews never run out of butter or booze. Bye."

The doorbell rings over the chatter and laughter of the other two families from school lounging around the appetizers. Dana steps around a kid wobbling on a balance board.

When she opens the door, sunlight pours in around her father. He has less hair combed over his bald spot. It's been four years. He hands her five pounds of butter. Instead of taking it, she embraces him. An unusual bloom unfurls in her chest: love, despair, disappointment, loyalty, anger, relief. It's complicated, but it's a flower nonetheless. The embrace is brief; Brooks and Elisa squeal and shove in. Dana closes the windows by the door so her neighbors won't overhear the prayers.

The Orcs of the Earth

Joseph J. Ridgway

The Orcs of the Earth
are not foreign
to the home
of the free
and the brave,
feasting upon
our freedoms,
driven by a cowardly
inability to trust,
devouring
our beautiful differences,
only to vomit
them back,
as alien
to their
bland and
comforting menu,
their pockets filled
with fools' gold,
dragging them under
nature's waves,
beneath the fresh air
we all seek to breathe.

Rash Writes This Poem During the Broken Night

Laura E. Garrard

I dream I had already composed this poem,
even seeing its form, its message of hope.
I'll read it to them today, I think in daylight,
then panic through shingles pain,
I haven't written a poem
                      about light.

I will describe how we survive this time
as stinging blisters pronounce
then flatten into red flames,
as lightning travels across my back,
and gray exhaust clouds neuron trees that gasp.
Anger burns then passes, grief over betrayal
by stabbing patches of activated virus.

I have no control, in floods sadness.
Oh my home, my country.
Danger skips rationale and invades
my body, the canary.
I pound the wailing drum,
purge heat into song, scream

               into light

                                          into light
                      into light

where the dark recesses brighten in the blast,
pain intensifies so that it curbs itself.
It is so radiant, we quiet, still, all agape, step back.
There is nothing more powerful,

        this light

                                                this light
              this light

penetrates our dread, overexposes,
none of us identified any longer
as this or that, we are now

        this light
            this light.

Oh my God, take our collective hands,
help us endure through our endeavors.
We surrender our pain.
We write. We abide in
                    this light.

A Revision

Korkut Onaran

A prophet,
(who looks like a rabbit),

protests God who orders him
to take his people and walk

into a new land currently occupied
by non-believers.

The prophet
foresees the bloodshed

and, to God's surprise,
he adopts another god;

a more modest
and peaceful one.

Can he do that?
He does it.

Crash Course
Kirk Astroth

Like a whirligig. Hikers on the ground said we spun around 10–12 times before we crashed. What I remember most, right before we crashed, was that the helicopter was doing this wild, whirling-dervish-type dance in the air, spinning, bucking, and diving, like we were riding a mechanical bull in a cowboy bar, before flipping and smashing into the rocks.

The crash took seconds; getting out seemed like forever. We knew enough to run like hell. Then, like gawkers at a disaster scene, the three of us stood there, looking back on the smashed and smoldering helicopter we had just escaped from, waiting for it to burst into flames. Nothing was moving, the fiberglass rotor shattered into a thousand pieces on impact. Smoke billowed from the turbine engine, and the acrid smell of jet fuel filled the air. My hands were sweating, my heart racing.

Standing there atop Mt. Baldy in Utah a hundred yards away from the crash, all three of us were frozen in place—mute, stunned, catatonic. Mere minutes before, the three of us had scrambled out of the wreckage and knew we had only minutes to spare. We were in a race against death.

Two years later, after all the depositions and a court trial, when I learned why we crashed, all I could think was, "Goddammit! Those bastards could've killed us!"

When I started working as a wildland firefighter with the Forest Service at age 19, I had no idea that I would be required to enter a sacrifice zone, to offer myself up as an expendable minion in the machinery of fire suppression and corporate profit. Young men and fire, a tangled web of hubris, naivete, and danger. Really, I guess I should have known better, but I was young and felt invincible. Dying never seemed remotely possible.

Fire is fascinating. Like many kids, I loved to play with fire. I burned all kinds of stuff. I enjoyed campfires. But I also found the destructive power of fires mesmerizing. Fires were hypnotic, transfixing, almost otherworldly, especially in the outdoors. The sweet smell of wood smoke, crackling branches in the firepit, airborne embers sailing into the night, the warmth of coals that could ward off the cold. Those orange flames, tinged with blue and yellow, licking the air and bouncing around were hypnotic, almost animal-like.

So, perhaps it was fate that I would find that fighting wildland fires was in my blood. After graduating from high school, I started applying for jobs with the Forest Service. And from my first job with the Wasatch National Forest, I loved it—the challenge, the camaraderie of the fire crews, the adrenaline rush, the danger, and even the grittiness of it all. This was the life I lived for eight seasons with the US Forest Service and then later with the Bureau of Land Management (BLM). It was why I kept coming back for more. I was young and in love—with fighting fires. We used to brag that firefighters like us were modern-day folk heroes, and heroes didn't die.

For several summers, I was the helitack foreman at BLM's Western Slope Fire Operations in Grand Junction, Colorado. WSFO was an interagency and interregional fire suppression base that included not only our helitack crew but also tanker planes that dropped retardant on fires. It's dangerous work and not a few people have died in the line of duty. Yet, I was certain I would never be one of them.

One day in early August, our helitack crew received orders to fly to the Mirror Lake area of the High Uintas in eastern Utah. Our role was to provide support to a large project fire that had broken out after a huge lightning storm had passed through the area several days before. Helicopters and fixed-wing aircraft used in firefighting are under private contract with the government, but as helitack foreman, I was the crew boss for our initial attack team and the lead person on the aircraft representing the federal government, responsible for seeing that we followed safety and operational protocols.

We landed at the fire camp heliport in a meadow after our flight from Grand Junction, and then set up our camp. Soon, the fire boss came around and said, "I need you to fly up to the top of Mt. Baldy with a radio tech so we can put up a radio tower in order to get communications with the main fire office down in Salt Lake City." It was early morning, cool temperatures, and a calm day. Sure, we could do that. Piece of cake. As helitack foreman for the crew, I quickly calculated our weight and consulted the flight charts to make sure that we could safely land at the top of the mountain at those temperatures and with our weight.

Off we went into the air. The day was beautiful, and it was early enough that there were no people yet on top of Mt. Baldy. The mountain has a popular hiking trail only 2 miles long that provides incredible vistas for miles around. Everything went like clockwork—we were able to land easily on the extensive boulder field that is common on the tops of peaks in the Uintas. While Wayne (the pilot) kept the chopper running, the radio tech, Kenny, and I got out and set up the radio tower, made sure it was working properly, got back in the ship, and flew back down to the fire camp.

But several hours later, the fire boss was back, saying, "The repeater station quit working. You need to go back up there and see what's wrong and fix it. We need that for communications into Salt Lake City."

But by now the weather was warmer, and the wind had picked up as it usually does in the mountains in the afternoons. And Mt. Baldy, at nearly 12,000 feet, can be very windy as the slopes heat up and air starts rising and moving around.

Instead, I suggested an alternative: "Send that Alouette Lama helicopter—it is better designed to land in boulder fields like the one on top of Mt. Baldy, and besides it has better performance at higher altitudes." I pointed out to him that Alouette Lama copters also have rubber wheels instead of rigid metal skids like our chopper, so these Alouette helicopters are often used for high-altitude work in rocky terrain.

"No," he said. "You've been up there already, so I want you to go."

I thought about it for a second. "Not me. I don't think it's safe and I won't go."

Then Wayne piped up. "Well, I'm not going unless he goes."

An awkward silence ensued, with glances all around. I couldn't abandon Wayne—he was my pilot and friend after an entire summer of fighting so many fires together. He couldn't fly without me on board.

"OK—I guess I'm going," I said, relenting under the pressure. We offloaded some fuel back into the fuel truck to make the aircraft lighter since we still also had to take the radio tech up with us again. Warmer air is thinner than cold air and a helicopter can't land carrying as much weight in warmer temps. I was not happy with how this had turned out, but I really didn't see a choice since the pilot wanted to go. He couldn't go without a helitack foreman.

When all was ready, we took off again for the top of Mt. Baldy. As we approached the top, I could see that there was a large group of people there, taking in the spectacular views from the summit. I leaned out my window and tried to signal that they needed to move off the center of the top so we could land.

We made a wide circle and came back on a final approach, nose into the south wind, and began a slow, gradual descent toward the area where the radio tower was located. The hikers moved off farther to the east.

Our helicopter, with its metal skids for landing, does poorly in boulder fields like the one we were trying to land on. It is critical that the back of the skids, where quite a bit of the weight of the aircraft is distributed, stays level, and can't roll backwards after landing. This can happen if the skids are over a hole and the whole ship can tilt backwards, allowing the tail rotor to strike the ground, something that—needless to say—would be disastrous.

As we got closer to the ground, the pilot said over the headset, "Kirk, lean out your door and spot my skids and make sure I'm not over a hole."

I opened my door, but my seatbelt restricted me from leaning out far enough, so I had to unbuckle my seatbelt and harness. The rotor was spinning at 2,000 revolutions per minute.

Before I could really get a good look toward the rear of the ship and see if we were safe to land, Wayne suddenly screamed over the headset: "Close the fucking door!!"

Instantly, I sat up and closed my door and then looked over at him to see why. Out of the corner of my eye, I saw that Kenny, the radio tech in the back seat, had opened his door and he was trying to get out of the helicopter while we were still up in the air. I grabbed him by his shirt and screamed, "Close that fucking door. What the fuck are you doing?" He just stared at me, panic shooting from his eyes. Mine were raging. He closed the door and sat back.

That's when I noticed that we were spinning, wobbling, and shuddering wildly in the air as if riding a bucking Brahma bull at a rodeo. I could see Wayne was wrestling with the rotor controls, but we started spinning in a tight circle, nose to the ground, when we suddenly flipped upside down, crashing onto the rocks on Wayne's side of the copter. It was over in seconds but seemed interminable.

In the crash, without my seatbelt on, I was catapulted across the console and landed on Wayne, knocking him temporarily unconscious. I knew I had to act quickly. Since the chopper was lying on its right side, I had to climb up to open my door, which opened to the sky. I looked around just to be sure that the rotor wasn't moving. Next, I dropped back down inside and got Wayne revived by screaming at him to get out: "Wayne! Get up! We've got to get out quick!" He roused himself, unbuckled from his seatbelt, shut off the engine, and climbed up over the console, over my seat, and out into the open air. The radio tech was next. He did the same scramble over the console from the back seat. Then it was my turn—working as quickly as I could to get out onto the helicopter skids, I jumped to the ground and got away from what would likely be a fiery mess in a few seconds.

Miraculously, the helicopter never caught fire. It just lay there on the rocks, like a dead dragonfly whose wings were broken and shattered. There were pieces of the main rotor scattered across the top of the mountain, blue fiberglass shards peppering the rocks. All three of us just stood there on the rocks looking at the helicopter, its engine smoking but otherwise eerily serene for what seemed like hours. The people behind us who had been where we landed just minutes before were crying, shouting, and a few were praying. For me, it was just so much gibberish to comprehend at that moment of extreme emotions. Insensitively, I screamed, "Get the hell out of here—that thing could explode any minute!" One of the men who was on his knees praying suddenly grew frightened, eyes as big as saucers, jumped up, and ran in the opposite direction.

It was a miracle that we didn't kill everyone on top of the mountain that day. We could have chopped up everyone with the wildly spinning rotor and the shrapnel that was thrown around when the rotor disintegrated. But fate would be on the side of those hikers that day. Our helicopter was made in France, an Aerostar 350, and those rotors are not only fiberglass, but they spin clockwise. Had we been in an American-made helicopter, where the rotors spin counter-clockwise, we would have rolled over the other direction when we flipped and landed right on top of all those hikers off to our left. As it was, we went to the right. And so, people did not die.

After several minutes, knowing that everyone was okay on the top of the mountain, I knew that I needed to call down to fire camp and let them know what happened. So, I radioed down with my handheld unit and said, "Helicopter 241 is out of commission," or some such euphemism. "Over." We were trained to never say "crashed" over the radio network.

"What?" comes the reply.

"Our helicopter is down and out of commission. Over." A long pause ensued.

Soon, I heard a response on my radio: "We're sending up another ship to get you. Over."

"No, I wouldn't recommend that. The winds are strong up here and its hot. Over."

Another long pause. Meanwhile, Wayne came over and told me, "I'm not walking down from here. Tell them to bring up another helicopter. I'll ride it down."

"OK, that's fine but I think I will walk down. It's not that far, there's a good trail that I have hiked many times, and right now I can't get in another helicopter."

"That's fine for you," Wayne says, "but I am not walking down in these cowboy boots."

I radioed back down to fire camp and told them to send up another helicopter—the Lama. The one with the rubber wheels that are designed to land in the rocks at high elevations. The helicopter I had originally recommended.

Within five minutes, we heard the helicopter's wop-wop sound, and it soon appeared over the horizon. It made a couple of passes to figure out how to land well away from the smoking wreckage, and then came down north of our position. Wayne boulder-hopped over to the chopper, got in, and off they flew back to fire camp.

Meanwhile the radio tech and I started hiking down the trail. I was grim and silent, but internally I was seething. "You asshole, you almost killed us. Why the fuck did you open that door?"

"I was scared. I knew something was wrong."

"I told you that you were to NEVER get out of the helicopter on your own. By opening your door, the wind probably caught it and caused Wayne to lose control and spin us around. You could have killed us all—even all those people on top."

The rest of the hike down was a silent retreat. At the trailhead, I radioed fire camp and asked someone to come up with a truck and pick us up. Within a half hour, we were back at fire camp and all eyes were on us. Survivors yet tainted with disaster.

Three days after the FAA incident team had completed their investigation, we returned to Grand Junction, but the scene was grim and somber. Without a helicopter, a helitack crew is like a cowboy without a horse. The rest of the crew that had stayed behind was now out of their jobs. Since it was August, most of us would be heading off to other jobs soon anyway as the fire season was coming to a close (small consolation)— me to graduate school at Utah State University, others to various occupations that would carry them through the fall and winter until fire season positions opened again next spring.

Partway through the next year, though, I got a call from a lawyer with a firm in Oregon where the helicopter company had its headquarters. They wanted to take a deposition from me about the wreck. Apparently, the wreck was going to litigation for damages of lost income to the helicopter company because of the crash. They were looking for deep pockets to recoup some of that lost income and the destroyed chopper. As the sole government employee in the lead role of helitack foreman on the helicopter, I was a key culprit in their case against the US government. What I didn't know, however, is that I was being set up as the fall guy.

In March of that year, a team of three lawyers rolled into Logan, UT, where I was going to school, to take my deposition for the lawsuit. I arrived at the appointed time and place to find them all seated, decked out in suits and ties, huge notebooks and legal pads on the table, and a court reporter in the corner with one of those Stenotype transcription machines.

It was 10:00 in the morning, and the questioning began after I was sworn in "to tell the truth, the whole truth"—you know the drill. At first the questioning was normal enough—where were you on August 10th, how long have you been doing this, what training did you have to be helitack foreman, who was your boss, what was your standard procedure for creating flight manifests, and the like. The questioning went on for two hours, the court reporter transcribing everything, and finally we broke for lunch.

After the break, we all reassembled in the small room and the questioning continued. I felt like I was having to recall and relive the eight summers I had spent firefighting—something I had not prepared myself mentally to have to recall in detail.

After a time, it began to dawn on me, given the nature and direction of their questioning, that they were trying to establish that I had inadequate training and experience in working as a helitack foreman for the BLM and that something I had done—like overloading the helicopter— had caused the wreck. I was still fixated on the radio tech having opened the rear door with strong winds, thinking that this had caused the accident. But I could tell that I was being set up to take the blame. The air between us was taut.

Eventually, late in the afternoon, the lead attorney pulled out a chart and put it in front of me. "According to this chart, you were only able to carry 825 pounds at that altitude and temperature that day, but your manifest shows that you were carrying a total of 1,250 pounds. How do you explain that?"

I looked at the photocopy of my manifest form for the flight, and then at the chart they had put in front of me. I looked back again at my manifest. And then back again to the chart. They seemed to be right—the weight limit we carried was more than what the chart indicated was safe. I was baffled and couldn't understand why. I kept looking back and forth at the two pieces of paper, trying to grasp why this didn't make sense.

And then I saw it—they had taken the "out-of-ground" effect chart from the helicopter manual and had been using that to make their case. Helicopters come with two sets of charts—"out-of-ground" and "in-ground" effect. One chart is used if you plan to hover some distance above the ground so that you don't have the benefit of the pillow or cushion of air created by the downwash of the rotor blades. This is the "out-of-ground" effect—you don't get a boost from the air bouncing off the ground and coming back up to buoy the helicopter—so you can't carry as much weight. This chart is used, for example, if you are long-lining a payload in a net, letting people rappel down ropes to a site, or other hovering maneuvers like dipping a large bucket into a lake to douse flames.

"In-ground" effect is when you are close enough to the ground to take advantage of the pillow of air created by the action of the rotors that allows you to carry more weight than simply hovering up in the air far above ground—typically a distance greater than the diameter of your rotor blades. This "pillow" of air created by the downwash of the rotors means you can carry more than when you are operating "out of ground."

So, I realized—these attorneys really didn't know anything about the mechanics of how helicopters worked, or they were trying to trick me, or trying to see if I really knew what I was doing. Either way—I knew that they were chasing a rabbit down the wrong hole. And I told them so.

"You have the wrong chart. You have the out-of-ground effect chart. We were operating in ground. Give me that other in-ground chart and let's see what it says that I could have been carrying."

"In ground? Out of ground? What are you talking about?"

"Please just hand me the helicopter manual," I pleaded.

The lead attorney opened the helicopter manual, and I found the other chart. I looked across the graph for elevation and temperature, and it showed we could have carried 1,500 pounds that day—we were well under the weight limit by a couple hundred pounds.

Once I showed this to them, and compared it to my manifest form, they all became very quiet.

"Thank you very much for your time today. That will be all." They hurriedly packed up their notebooks and legal pads, put away their pens, the court reporter closed the top of her Stenograph machine, and they quickly left the room, saying, "We will be in touch."

By June of that year, I got a subpoena to appear in US District Court in Portland, Oregon, to testify in the trial about the helicopter wreck. When my turn came, I entered the court room with the BLM lawyer and proceeded to take a seat in the witness stand. This was a judge trial, not a jury trial, so there was just me, the lawyers for both sides—the helicopter company and the US government—and the judge and a court reporter present in the courtroom.

The lawyers for the helicopter company began, again, with many of the very same questions they had asked me in Logan when I gave my deposition in March. They wanted me to repeat my background in firefighting and my training as a helitack foreman. I repeated what I told them before. I suppose the purpose of this was to see if my two versions were consistent. Blame is a spiteful, bitter experience.

As before, the questioning went on seemingly forever. This time, too, they brought out the charts from the helicopter manual and asked me how I calculated the weight limit that we could fly with that day. I repeated the difference between in-ground and out-of-ground effect charts and told them that we were flying "in-ground" so we could carry more weight than the other chart indicated.

And then that was it. "No more questions, your Honor."

My government attorney then approached the stand and asked, "In your opinion, what caused the crash?"

"I thought that when the radio tech opened the rear door to try and get out before we had fully set down it caused the wind to catch his door and forced us into a spin, and then the crash."

"Anything else?"

"No."

"That's all my questions, your Honor."

And then I was excused. I left the courtroom with my government lawyer, and outside the courtroom, he thanked me for testifying and said that he would be in touch after everyone had testified and a judgment had been reached.

Two months later, I got a call from my government attorney. After the perfunctory greetings and small talk, he said, "I have some news to share with you about the trial. The helicopter company was found liable for negligence. They had tried to save money and were not performing the required regular maintenance on the helicopter all summer. As a result, the rear bearings in the tail rotor failed, which is what caused the helicopter to spin out of control and crash."

"What? Are you serious?" I couldn't believe it. The tail rotor is what keeps the helicopter on a straight trajectory or can help turn the ship in different directions, depending on the torque that is put on the rotor blades. If the bearings fail, it is like having a wheel fall off your car. I was in shock—and angry. It wasn't the radio tech opening the door at all that caused the crash. And it wasn't because of my weight calculations. It was the helicopter company. They put profits ahead of human lives. I had become a pawn in the blame game. "Goddammit! Those bastards did try to kill us!" I was livid with a rage that knew no bounds, a rage that grew like an internal conflagration, consuming every other emotion in its path.

That day in June, after I heard the news about the court judgment in Portland, I walked around in circles in my Logan apartment, experiencing a multitude of thoughts, emotions, and reactions, mumbling to myself like a delirious mental case. While I was relieved to hear the news, I was also inconsolable. Deep inside, I could sense that I needed to find some sort of resolution between rage and redemption. I knew I needed to find a way out of my anger.

I had been lucky, that I knew. But I had had too many dangerous close calls in the past while fighting fires—fire blowups, landings in foggy conditions, back-burns gone wrong, getting splattered and knocked down by fire retardant dropped by planes flying at 125 miles per hour. I even had to deploy my "turkey tent" far too many times on previous fires. Too many friends I knew had died in "burn overs," truck wrecks, and aircraft crashes. I knew now that I was fortunate not to have been one of them. I was lucky to have escaped death so many times.

Until you stare your own death directly in the face, thoughts of death or dying are unreal—fake even. Until you confront the real possibility of your own death, like twirling around in a helicopter atop a 12,000-foot mountain, your own mortality dwells in the land of fantasy. But this time, I had entered a tragicomedy, stage left, forced to play a part in life's drama. Fortunately, I failed my audition with Death that summer—again.

I needed to find a way to process my anger at being led like a lamb into a sacrifice zone that so many firefighters and pilots had not survived. Serenity within the four walls of my apartment was impossible. I needed to get outside and sit somewhere, processing all these rapid-fire emotions and thoughts. I recalled the wisdom of C.S. Lewis: "I sat with my anger long enough until she told me her real name was grief." Getting outside seemed the only way to put everything in perspective and achieve some sort of resolution if not closure at all of what I had lost.

Despite a steady drizzle of rain that day, I decided to hike to one of my favorite locations in Logan Canyon. The Jardine juniper is the oldest Rocky Mountain juniper tree in the world, variously estimated to be as much as 3,000 years old. It is impossible to look at this ancient tree and not admire its ability to survive. St. George observed that "what most arouses the inner philosopher is not a tree's size or shape or ubiquity but their age." Trees form a bridge beyond the usual human experience. The 5-mile trail lends itself to contemplation and reflection, especially in a gentle rain. I was so consumed with anger that I barely remembered the hike.

Once at the juniper, though, its gnarled, twisted trunk and ancient limbs inspired a sense of respect and wonder. What resilience and persistence it conveyed. After many minutes of sitting in quiet contemplation beneath its branches, I imagined that the juniper whispered a message of hope to calm my rage. It was a message from a being grounded in centuries of lived experiences of fortitude and resistance.

From this unspoken message, I knew that it was time to do something different with my life. It was clear now to me— my career fighting fires was over. I realized, that unlike me, there weren't a lot of people over 30 years old still doing this kind of work. And even though I was going to school at Utah State to get a degree in natural resources so that I could work full-time for the Forest Service or BLM, that no longer seemed viable or even possible.

I needed to find a way to move beyond the rage and recrimination I felt at everything that had happened. Time to choose a different path. I would need to find new ground, put down new roots, and steel myself to weather the storms and tempests of the future as this ancient juniper had done for so many decades. My pass/fail crash course in life's lessons was at an end.

I retraced my steps back the way I had come to reach the old juniper. One step at a time, I returned to Logan Canyon and back to the hope of new possibilities.

I never set foot in another helicopter again.

Marines Don't Cry

Larry Chrysler

I'd only been in California a few weeks. I was 19, full of that restless energy you have when you think life is just about to start—and then it slaps you in the face.

The slap arrived in the form of a special delivery letter from the Military Induction Center.

"Report in a few weeks," it said.

Welcome to Hollywood.

The morning I showed up at the downtown LA Induction Center, the air smelled of diesel buses and burnt coffee. Inside, the place echoed with orders barked by men in khaki. Before I knew it, we were stripped naked, standing shoulder-to-shoulder in a circle with 30 other guys, skin goose-pimpled in the air-conditioned chill. A stocky sergeant with a jaw like a meat cleaver strolled in and bellowed, "One outta fifteen of you is going to the Marine Corps."

Guess what number I was? Yeah—15.

My knees wobbled. I honestly thought I might faint. Later, when I called my parents to break the news, my mother dropped the phone. Literally. My father's voice came on, steady but strained: "We'll be praying for you, son."

A few hours later, they herded us onto a bus headed for San Diego. I ended up next to a guy from Finland who'd enlisted to get his US citizenship. His English was choppy. But fear is its own language. We bonded quick.

Up and down the aisle, a drill instructor paced like a caged tiger, screaming about how we were about to be transformed into Killer Marines. His voice rattled the metal frame of the bus.

"You'd better shape up fast," he roared.

So, we shaped up. We sat there like statues carved from pure terror the rest of the ride.

I made myself a promise: If this is a game, I'm going to learn the rules.

And I did.

Boot camp was brutal—sand in your teeth, muscles screaming, boots that felt like they'd been designed for someone with hooves. But after two weeks, I'd cracked the code. Swagger when you walk. Curse like punctuation. Wear your fatigues like a second skin.

Then came Captain Mercer.

One morning in formation—Dress Right Dress—heads turned right, left hands on hips, eyes straight ahead. Captain Mercer strolled behind me and murmured, almost casually, "You look like you should be wearing furs and draped in jewels."

I didn't flinch. Just stared ahead, my face a mask. But my Finnish buddy heard him, and we christened him Captain Mabel Mercer. The nickname stuck.

Six weeks later, against all odds, I graduated. Private First Class.

Camp Pendleton was my next stop, just south of Laguna Beach. My assignment? Clerk in the Supply Department. I handed out rifles, uniforms, and sometimes boots two sizes too small. It was a nine-to-five job—if your office job came with the smell of gun oil and the constant reminder that your paperwork might send someone to war.

Fridays at 5:00 a.m., we'd issue rifles to green Marines being shipped to Korea. Most of them didn't know they were heading straight into the Battle of Bunker Hill. Watching them climb onto those trucks, joking and smoking like they were going on a camping trip, made me start praying in earnest: Please, God, don't send me to Korea.

During Friday roll call, some joker would always shout, "Hey, you guys going up to movie producer George Cukor's place for the weekend? Free beer and chow!"

Tempting? Sure. But I knew better. "Nah," I'd yell back, "got other plans." Truth was, I was scared they'd find out I was gay. If they did, I wouldn't be yelling anything ever again.

And the straight guys? Some of them had no problem getting . . . let's just say . . . serviced. "Not gay," they'd insist. Right. Keep telling yourself that.

One morning at the PX, I spotted a tall, blond, tan guy behind the coffee counter. Surfer's shoulders. A smile that looked like it had been bleached by the California sun. I knew him instantly from volleyball games at Will Rogers Beach, back before camouflage became my daily wardrobe.

His name was Al. Pasadena guy. We reintroduced ourselves, laughed at the coincidence, and met that night for drinks at a little bar in Laguna.

Sparks flew. Lust, not love—let's be honest. We didn't have much in common, but proximity breeds passion, especially when your world is defined by barracks, reveille, and the sound of boots on gravel.

Weekends became our escape: cheap motels in Laguna, quiet stretches of sand at Dana Point, salt air in our lungs, and the low hum of waves drowning out the rest of the world. Our secret.

But secrets don't stay secrets.

One day, we were summoned to the Colonel's office. A gay sailor had broken up with his Marine boyfriend, and in a fit of revenge, he started naming names. Mine. Al's. Others.

They interrogated us in separate rooms. They had motel names. Dates. Details. They offered me a deal: Admit it, name others, and I'd get a quiet discharge. They even promised not to tell my parents I was a "homo."

I told them nothing.

Others weren't so lucky—or so silent. It snowballed. Chaplains, nurses, navy personnel—over 120 discharged. No lawyers. No hearings. Just men and women marched to the brig, their lives stripped bare.

I joined them. My new home: a five-by-eight-foot concrete cell with a thin mattress and a metal toilet. The highlight of my day? Marching to the mess hall under a big sign that read "WOMEN MARINES." Hilarious—to everyone else.

After a few weeks, they let me out and sent me back to the same tent with five guys. Four of them hugged me.

"Are you okay?" they asked.

I gave the standard answer, the one that covers everything and nothing: "No, really, I'm fine."

Then came the day. The "undesirables" were ordered to wear our dress uniforms and battle ribbons. We stood on the parade field, every eye on us. The general walked down the line, stopping in front of each man.

When he reached me, he grabbed my ribbons and ripped them from my chest.

It felt like he was tearing out my heart.

I stood still. Eyes forward. Marines don't cry.

Years later, flipping through the *LA Times*, I read that Al had died. I pictured his sunburned nose, the golden hair on his legs, and the way his laugh rose above the crash of the waves.

It hit me harder than I expected.

And then, finally, I cried.

I took a deep breath. Wiped my eyes.

But . . . no, really, I'm fine.

Going Infinite

Nathaniel Phillips

The only way out is through
Heard it many times but I never knew
I would write my own reality
Creation is the only escape
from separation, and finality
And I would make it
With sweat and preparation
Words shaping worlds and generations

Then the SPRT was a mirror
Went and hit me with the future
Straight up struck me with instructions
Now I'm laughing
While I'm snacking
On a muffin.
Once the yeast
Was discomfort
Now it's ripe
With the light
Of a star filled with life
A path to follow into nothing
As if nothing wasn't something
Now I'm buzzing.
Brain abundant,
With a method of construction
Though the branch is hollow

I've been shown a
Way to give it marrow
With tomorrow

Now in the past,
This feat was seen
As an impossible task
Now it's a probable path
This time though, the blow
Missed my moneymaker
It was more like,
Right on the top of the head
Open palm to my crown
Now All Along . . .
Had I been drinking
Vegetable juice
Instead of lead poison
Bled from refuse
I'd be next to you
So much closer
To unfolding
The inherent nature;
Of being, Children of Stars
Descendants from cosmic parents
Who wrap all of their babies
In grace and favor
Without limits or scars
This lineage is all of OURS

The Multiverse

M.J. Simmering

In the multiverse of verse,
there are no immutable laws.

In one universe,
we meet at 15.
You run along the streets, thudding,
still knobby kneed,
as cataclysm chases catechism
through your veins.
I pass you,
lost in a daydream about a blue-eyed drummer
who one day will remember
my name but little else.

In another universe,
we meet at 52.
My runaway shopping cart
bumps the door of your Subaru.
In the midst of parking lot hash marks,
you are grizzled and grumpy;
I am crampy and combative.
I am an irritant and you
are another mistake I have made.

In another universe,
we meet at 23 at a Bowie concert,
tipsy if not fully baked.
In the back of an unlicensed cab,
I stardust your ziggy
as we speed up the West Side Highway.
We watch as a Tesla is launched into space,
and a mannequin driver listens to Starman
on endless repeat.
We do not understand gravity and the pull of blackholes.

In another universe,
we meet at conception—
me the sperm and you the egg
or possibly the other way around.
As each cell divides and multiples,
we create zygotic poems
until we enter the world
soft skulled and hungry.
We are unstoppable.

In another universe,
we meet at 30,
hiking on a woodland trail.
We find a jack-in-the-pulpit,
growing in the shade,
and kneel before it.
Our ragged breaths
are the only vows we take.
We lie down
and become as green
as emeralds.

And in this universe,
we meet at 60
and share an apple, already
peppered with cider-sweet bruises.
Each knotted vein
finds its companion,
shuttling blood
back to the heart.
We send each other poems,
weaving words together.
What are we creating?
A tapestry? A blanket? Another noose?

There is one thing you must understand.

In the multiverse of verse,
there is one immutable law:
everything in a poem is true,
but not everything
is real.

You Remind Me

Ross Berger

You remind me of my grandson . . .

said the Old Man by the pool table. He watched me scratch on the first break, and when he took over, he cleared the table, one ball at a time. There was a tremor in his right hand, just slight. His hand was so beefy it didn't matter; he owned the cue like a backroom hustler.

"My grandson used to come here to play with me," the Old Man said. "I told his father he's got one helluva break." He then gingerly knocked the 8-ball into a side pocket.

"He stopped visiting after a while," said the Old Man. "He got a car for his sixteenth birthday. Drove it to impress the girls."

I racked up the balls for the next game. "My grandson calls me every Christmas, every Easter," said the Old Man. He stopped smiling. "He's young. Like you."

We leaned over the table and lagged for the break. The Old Man didn't bother to see which ball was the closest to the innermost edge of the head cushion. He won the lag, but, like a good grandpa, offered me the break.

He then grabbed both my cheeks and when his smile returned, the Old Man told me,

You remind me of my grandson . . .

You remind me of my brother . . .

said the Attractive Woman, holding her new husband by her side. "He died not that long ago," she said. "You look so much like him; it's scary."

We both laughed at the awkwardness, and then I told her it was nice meeting her before heading toward the gridlock of the party. I waved goodbye to be polite; she stared at me. As I mingled with others, the Attractive Woman followed me, skulking in the background, trying not to be seen and trying to be seen.

When I chatted up a friend, the Attractive Woman interrupted me and told me again how the resemblance to her brother was uncanny. She touched my chin and smiled dotingly. "He was two years older than me," the Attractive Woman said. "I miss him so much." I excused myself to use the bathroom and, on the way, asked another friend to shield me in case the Attractive Woman started following me again.

The evening went on for a few hours more, and I saw her leave with her husband. Drunk, she stumbled to the ground and made a scene. Her husband threw up his hands in defeat and took a few steps backward. I walked over and helped her up.

The Attractive Woman then hugged me and held onto my shoulders tightly. When she spoke, one could smell the fresh misery from the back of her throat. "I miss him so much," the Attractive Woman repeated, "I miss him so much . . ."

She lingered on my hand when her husband escorted her to the door. She waved goodbye, a tear down her cheek, in a stupor but not lost, and whispered,

You remind me of my brother . . .

You remind me of David . . .

said the New Neighbor. "David Cohen. We used to work together. He probably belongs to the same Church as you," he said. "Do you know him?"

I said no but I don't go to Church, and I doubt David Cohen does either. The New Neighbor moved in closer. "You a lawyer?" No, I said, without eye contact, signaling the end of the conversation, or so I thought. When he didn't budge, I told him I didn't have a job at the time, was renting a friend's Florida home for the summer, a rash decision to get out of dodge. "To live in this town, you must be good with money then," said the New Neighbor. I nodded pro forma, smiling, but in fear.

He'd invite me to go fishing, to go hunting, to go to NASCAR. All of which I turned down. The invitations stopped coming. Whenever I pulled into my driveway, he was either mowing his lawn or hosing down his Range Rover. We'd wave at each other. That, too, stopped after a while.

But when an intruder broke into my house, it was the New Neighbor who came to my side. Shotgun in hand, the New Neighbor scared off the intruder, who fled with my wallet and the broken Longines my grandfather gave me in high school. The New Neighbor steadied my trembling shoulders and nodded as I followed his confident eyes. "You're all good," said the New Neighbor. "You're all good." He put up his arm, 90 degrees, Rosie the Riveter style, and motioned that I do the same, to lock our hands in a sign of unity. Our grip led to a brief competition of flexed biceps. He won.

As we waited for the police, I told him this was the most physical contact I'd had in two years, "I should buy you dinner." He rolled with laughter and said,

You remind me of David . . .

You remind me of my father . . .

said the Lost One while we were being intimate. I was taken aback, as anyone would be in that moment, but I listened intently as I was just as lost as she was. "You're just so kind to me," she cried. "Why?"

I held her and kissed her on her neck. The Lost One rested her chin upon my left shoulder. When her breathing slowed down, she explained her in-and-out presence in my life, her defensiveness too. "I'm sorry I've been so cruel to you. I'm just so confused right now."

I told her it didn't matter. I was just happy to be with her. We shivered when the broken window in my Brooklyn studio let in the December air. I gave her an extra pair of sweatpants, which were three sizes too big for her. The Lost One lay upon my belly as we watched black-and-white movies 'til midnight.

She got up the next morning, ordered French toast from a nearby diner, and declared her love for me. She then tied up her snow boots, donned her peacoat over my sweatpants, gently closed the door behind her, and never came back. I finally got in touch with her a month later. "How was the French toast?" The Lost One apologized and told me she can't be with anyone right now, especially with someone like me.

"Why not?" I asked.

You remind me of my father . . .

You remind me of a wolf . . .

said the Older Lover, timid of the young, but wanting them all the same. "You're hairy like one, and you bite like one." Yet it was she who devoured me whole that day and then showed me off to all her divorced friends later that night. The next day, she paid for my $200 haircut and took me to a luxury department store to buy me clothes that made me look like an imposter, that made me look desperate.

I was new to the city, too busy barhopping, and suddenly found myself the object of relentless focus. The Older Lover kept calling me "Beautiful," even though I wasn't. But I was 25 and therefore young, and therefore beautiful enough.

When she called me during the week, she asked me what I was up to, what my workout was like, if I was thinking of her. When I wouldn't tell her, she wanted me even more.

During our clothing spree, I had bought myself a T-shirt to convey to the Older Lover that I, too, can afford expensive things. But the shirt was too lavish (and yes, too expensive), so I went to return it the following weekend. I bumped into her near men's shoes. She was pawing a younger man, younger than me, much more handsome than me, and was buying him clothes as well.

I confronted her and told her this isn't for me. The Older Lover feigned insult, told me I was cruel, and snarled:

You remind me of a wolf . . .

You remind me of my best friend . . .

said the Middle-Aged Lawyer, who just sued a client for not paying him for services rendered. The client happened to be the best man at his wedding, for a marriage that lasted just two years. The Middle-Aged Lawyer confided that the list of people close to him had dwindled to none. He found comfort in going to bars and meeting new people even though, he admitted, he never did.

One Sunday, the Middle-Aged Lawyer saw that I rooted for the same sports team as he did. We talked about James Harden's Euro-step, then Trump's deplorables, and finally Aaron Rodgers's delicate ego. We got drunk and after our sixth beer, he told me, "I have no one to talk to when I go home at night. Sometimes I sleep in my car so I don't have to face an empty bed."

I pressed my hand on his husky shoulder, grabbed its meat, and offered some drunken advice: "It's not the company you keep, but the company that keeps *you.*"

The Middle-Aged Lawyer eased into my fortune cookie wisdom. Inebriation helped; but the attention from a stranger was the stronger high. He gave me his card and told me to call him for another round of beers sometime soon. And when he headed for the exit, the Middle-Aged Lawyer had more to say but didn't or couldn't and momentarily froze, and in the charm and aimlessness of a first grader, told me,

You remind me of my best friend . . .

You remind me of my son . . .

said the Lady in Capri Pants, who, suffering from dementia, suddenly remembered the face of the boy she gave up when she was young. She had never seen him when he grew hair, or when he formed the true color of his eyes, but my warm smile was welcoming and sparked a maternal instinct that the Lady in Capri Pants hadn't felt, she said, since she was 17.

"I have lived my whole life not knowing who to care for," she said. She tried to rise from the park bench, but her attendant kept her still.

The Lady in Capri Pants grabbed my hand and asked me if I had led a good life. She relished my every syllable and raised her brow and opened her eyes as if I were her little boy who had just walked for the first time, or so she imagined.

When I said goodbye, the Lady in Capri Pants wouldn't let go of my hand.

"Don't leave," she said frantically. "Let's not leave each other again."

The attendant clutched her wrist and applied a little pressure until the Lady in Capri Pants slowly let go of me. As I walked away, her confusion was endless, and with it, also endless, her spoken refrain:

You remind me of my son . . .

You remind me of home . . .

said the Wife-to-Be. She was an Army brat, so I questioned if she even knew what home was. She simmered, let go of my hand, and walked in front of me along the boardwalk of the beach, refusing to look behind. After sunset, a swath of sunbathers rushed to their cars. A shirtless lardon of a man stepped on the big toe of the Wife-to-Be. The expected curse words followed. I re-grasped her hand and guided her to a bench.

"I may not have had a permanent zip code for more than two years," she said, bristling from either the stubbed toe or my flip remark, "but I know what home is."

I apologized, but the Wife-to-Be was not convinced: "Home is comfort. Home is protection. Home is routine."

"So, I'm routine?" I asked.

"Will you be there when I go to sleep every night, when I wake up the next morning?"

"Yes, always."

We locked eyes. She furrowed her brow and inspected me. She turned away and lay her body upon the bench, her head upon my lap. I stroked her hair until she fell asleep. I lost track of time and found the night easy to surrender to.

I awoke when the headlights of a passing van pinched my eye. I heard a small laugh below me. There she lay, the Wife-to-Be, a sideways vision of giggles and joy. You remind me of home, said the Wife-to-Be.

You remind me of home . . .

You are my home.

Frames

Ira Batra Garde

1. Unframed photographic portrait of my parents, Chester, England

My mother knits, stylishly slim and dressed in an elegantly draped silk *sari*, its sheen shimmering the sari's folds even through sienna shades of their photographic portrait.

My Indian father wears a Norwegian pullover sweater, reindeer crossing his chest, an engineering journal poised on his lap. His glasses are stern and intellectual, his face soft.

Neither looks at the task in their hands. They are in their poses, looking at one another, in their home in Chester, England. Their faint smiles tell me both see the other as beautiful.

In front of them, two Danish teacups rest on a table. The teacups look empty; they are posing too.

A framed photograph of me at two-and-one-half years of age rests between my parents on the heavy wooden dresser behind. They took me to a photography studio in Bombay before they left for England. They had the studio frame the photo. It was something for them to take to England, to remember me by.

They are on a work assignment with the Shell Oil Company in England. I am only there in the framed photograph, in which I am holding my favorite doll.

The unframed portrait of my parents in their Chester, England living room finds its way into an album rarely seen.

2. Snapshot of me when I am two-and-one-half years old, Chandigarh, India

While my parents are away in England, I inhabit the home of my grandparents and aunt in Chandigarh, "the house of the moon," Corbusier's planned city in northern India.

A snapshot taken of me there shows me as lost, a furrow of worry on my brow, as if frozen in response to the sharp glint of India's perpetual sun, a pout waiting for their return.

In the snapshot, I'm in the arms of my aunt. I'm told I would cling to my aunt, not let her go. I worried about never seeing her again, about losing her, too.

How long does a two-and-one-half-year-old child wait for her traveling parents until she feels lost emotionally? She will miss her parents, or those who have cared for her. She will "worry" that they will never return, that she will never see them again. For her, they have disappeared.

3. My parents return to India when I am four

They return to India one-and-one-half years later. This time, I lose my grandparents and aunt when I leave Chandigarh to live again with my parents in Bombay.

As I grow, I will smell my mother's French perfume. I'll notice her *teasing* her hair into a *bouffant*. I'll touch her favorite silk *sari*, the Danish teacups, and the Norwegian wool sweater, put away in a closet.

Their European tastes and the artifacts they collected during their one-and-one-half years in England tell me where they have been without me.

4. We emigrate from India to the United States when I am eight

Photographs accompany us.

Before we emigrate, they sell my favorite doll, whom I call by the name my grandmother had wanted for me: *Yukti*, derived from Sanskrit. I hold *Yukti* close in the framed photograph.

Now, I have only *Yukti's* photograph. I invoke her name, *Yukti.* The *Y* sound to start my name was important to my grandmother. It would support qualities she wanted for me: a strong personality; a drive to succeed; and a natural sense of leadership.

As I grow, in each home we inhabit, I see the framed photograph of me taken when I was two-and-one-half—on the fireplace mantle in Ridgewood, New Jersey; my father's desk in Houston, Texas; in Berkeley, California, atop a metal filing cabinet.

In all our houses, as we move and I grow, I look at the framed photograph of me clutching my doll, taken while I am still happy, before my parents left me and went away to England.

In the United States, I come to know the *sari* my mother wore in the portrait of my parents taken in England. It is raw silk. Its colors, a field of beige-brown with a contrasting *ikat* border in maroon, gold, and emerald-green, are sophisticated.

She drapes it perfectly when she goes out to a party. In the full-length mirror, she pouts her lipsticked lips. Her face is slim, her cheekbones high, before she leaves our home to attend a party.

5. Framed photograph of me, at two-and-one-half years, holding my doll, Berkeley, California

When I am a woman in my late thirties, with a daughter of my own, my parents prepare to sell their house in Berkeley and move to another.

I notice that the photograph of me has been moved from its usual place in my father's study. It is now hanging on the wall near the front door. Here, potential buyers of the house will see it.

I know my parents' reasoning: They've removed the Tibetan *mala* from the entry wall to protect it. My photograph is serving to fill the empty spot.

I am alarmed to find myself in so vulnerable a place. So, I take myself off the wall and carry her home. Now, we sit together in my study.

I listen to her—the betrayal, insecurity, loss, perpetual longing, frailty with goodbyes.

Reclaiming her was a beginning.

White Sneakers

Leah Channas

I swear I was over you until I got this gift card. You see, I want new white sneakers.

I once had a pair I liked; I once had a you I liked.

I look through old photos to remember what they looked like on me. Huh, they're not as I remember. Distorted, unflattering. I'm fairly certain they did not always look like that.

I see a photo of you. The hour hand sneaks four times around the sun before I realize I've searched through all of my old photos of you.

Panic flames my chest as I scan photo after photo in silent horror. I'm wearing the sneakers, but see, they're all wrong!

Your angular scowl, however, looks exactly as I remember— handsome, harsh, uncertain. It almost distracts me from noticing the sneakers are the wrong shade. They aren't even white! I panic-flip through a series of photos dated three years prior.

Clearly, some sort of wear-and-tear was the culprit for ruining the color. Maybe it was one of the countless treks across rain-drenched fields that etched permanent dis-coloration into the stitches, staining them. I remember the exact spot on the muddy corner where you first wrapped your hand around my throat; you laughed because we must have been play-fighting. I remember thinking this must be what raw, uncontrolled desire feels like, just like the movies.

The blurry karaoke nights could have been a factor, too. Mixed liquid mysteries sloshed over the sides of our plastic cups, inevitably splashing onto my beloved sneakers. It was probably the same night when you told me that you didn't know if you ever really loved your fiancée or if you only offered to marry her because she was dying. You trusted me with such a vulnerable thought. You cared so much! I think I was in love.

But if I squint just right, the shoes look devoid of any memories at all. A colorless gray.

And if I recall, I had white sneakers. These shoes aren't mine! There has to be a mistake.

What if I buy new sneakers and they come out all wrong again? I want white sneakers, not gray. Perhaps I can call the manufacturer, confirm my order. This time I will get exactly what I expect, no surprises.

I glance once more at a photo of the gaze I have burned into my soul. I know every groove, every mocking eye, every concealed smirk. And now I'm disillusioned by each one.

You wanted me to watch, you let me fall. But then you laughed—I could never keep any of the faces for myself. I wonder if you didn't like my sneakers.

I shake my head of the thought and throw the gift card into the trash. For some reason I won't bring myself to call the shoe company. I know that the order will be wrong, even if I do everything to make it right.

Search for the Survived

Amy Cook

Prologue

For some people, ancestry is an arrow that reaches back
through time and space, taut and direct. They can trace their
lineage to damn near the beginning of the civilized world. My
husband's line reaches back to the 16th century; stacks of
church documents and military records prove his ancestors'
existence. For the children of diaspora, children of slavery,
children of holocaust, our arrows bend and break. Like a
frayed string, or a broken body; connective tissue has been
removed. We spend our lives searching for clues.

A street corner, spring, 2023. Several months before
everything changes.

"You Jewish?"

It's Friday afternoon on the Upper West Side of
Manhattan, and the Mitzvah Tank is parked outside of
Trader Joe's. The Hasidic man asking me this is no more than
a boy; his beard and peyos age a tender face. I want to say,
Look at me. We are the same. Or at least, *shalom.* I don't. I
don't have time to daven in front of Trader Joe's, nor do I want
a free menorah. The last one was a fire hazard. And my cat has
asthma. No more candles.

Like most people, I'm wearing headphones, and when
approached by anyone, I keep walking. Because as much as I
can't slow down, I cannot say, "No, I'm not Jewish." Sometimes

I say, "No, thanks," answering an unasked question. Mostly, I say nothing, keeping my head down.

Still. The man/boy's voice is so familiar, his cadence the same as my great-grandmother's; she was a refugee of the deadly Lwów pogroms that predated the Holocaust by two decades. I can pick up this rhythm, too, the last vestiges of an old world. But Grandma Pauline spoke in a language she simply called Jewish. She meant by this Hebrew, English, Yiddish, Polish, German . . . bits of Ukrainian? Any language she picked up in the wandering. Her voice was filled with color and substance.

Most every Friday, walking around the neighborhood, I am asked if I am Jewish. Here, it's not a bad guess. I live in the bagel and lox capital of the world (save—maybe—the Lower East Side). Zabar's is just up the street. Pastrami Queen, too. On any given Shabbat morning, our avenues are filled with families walking to shul. It is no more unusual to see a man wearing a yarmulke than to see a runner heading to Central Park.

But it is in these moments, when I am asked who I am, I think about Pauline, who was as much a refugee as she was an immigrant. As an adult, Pauline was once scolded by a teacher, because her five-year-old daughter spoke several languages, but none of them were English. Pauline came to the United States at 17, accompanied by distant relatives, leaving behind a Jewish family that would be decimated by war. We were told, as children, not to ask about the lost. It was, my mother warned, too upsetting. It was hard for me to imagine, stuck as I was in my little girl world. I did not see.

I learned later on in life that Pauline's brother, Cousin "Simon," had escaped from some sort of camp. But for years, the details remained inaccessible. This was a man I had never met. In my forties, I learned about him and his wife, their child, and their harrowing attempt to escape with their lives. I know their story because he had the will to have it recorded. Like many courageous others, in the face of annihilation, in the raw dawn of a world, Szymon Wulwik, a man not yet 40, agreed to have his tale memorialized in the Register of Jewish Survivors.

I felt the weight of it, even before I started to read. Szymon and his family didn't have the choice to say, no, I'm not Jewish. They didn't keep walking.

Well, that's what I assumed.

I search for the connective tissue, wondering if it's still there.

1.

In the Holocaust Survivors and Victims Database, Cousin Szymon's testimony is summarized in the following language:

> The author, his wife and child escaped from the ghetto before its liquidation. He hid in Kraków, and later with his family in the village[s] of Kasinka Mała and Myślenice. He was denounced and held in prison in Kraków and in a labor camp in Skarżysko-Kamienna. He managed to escape and return to Kraków, where he and his wife lived to see the liberation (the child died in the ghetto in Bochnia).

The date of his testimony is March 23, 1947; the location given is a city in Poland called Wałbrzych, some 560 kilometers from his hometown of Sieniawa. It is two years after liberation. Wałbrzych itself had been home to several camps and prisons. So many people had been marked for death, but some still lived. Tried to live. In his papers, my cousin introduces himself to the world, "My spirit had crumbled."

Four words, trying to address a universe of grief and despair. Now, decades later, his American cousin pores over his fragile text; knowing, instinctively, that she is one of a handful of his readers. Cousin Szymon writes not contemporaneously but post facto, when the preservation of atrocity seemed the only way through it all. His testimony is quite different from the way many are used to viewing the Holocaust, in pictures.

Decades later, most Jews are familiar with the photographs and the film snippets of liberation, carefully documenting the debris of our grandparents' nightmares. What the soldiers found, when they came upon Auschwitz and Bergen-Belsen—Majdanek and Dachau. Piles of corpses. Mountains of shoes, glasses, business suits and . . . hair. Abandoned gas chambers; crematoriums. Those who had made it out alive had lived through days, weeks, months, *years* of being hunted, both by Nazis and the unforgiving diseases that ran rampant in camps with no sanitation. Their heads were shaved, their bodies merely skin that hung on hollow bones.

I watched those films for the first time when I was seven or eight, in Hebrew school. I was not unfamiliar with the idea of the Holocaust. Some of my friends had grandparents who still bore the ink from concentration camp tattoos; my aunt's parents were survivors, too. We were being asked to watch the footage, we were told, because we needed to see with our own eyes what had happened to our people. And we, our teachers warned, must never let this happen again.

I wondered if something was being lost in translation.

Did 6 million Jews walk, willingly, to their own deaths? And how could I, a mere *child,* do anything about it now?

In his book, *Crusade in Europe*, General Eisenhower wrote,

> I visited every nook and cranny of the camp because I felt it my duty to be in a position from then on to testify at first hand about these things in case there ever grew up at home the belief or assumption that "the stories of Nazi brutality were just propaganda." . . . I felt that the evidence should be immediately placed before the American and British publics in a fashion that would leave no room for cynical doubt.

Eisenhower does this not with text. Well, not just text. A photo, from the Eisenhower Library: "April 14, 1945—Pile of ashes and bones found by U.S. soldiers at Buchenwald concentration camp in Germany." The week before, when the Germans knew the Americans were coming, more than half of the camp, 28,000 prisoners, were removed, sent to their deaths.

Even the most cryptic photographs can be translated by the brain. Photography is an art, yes, but an art that captures our world as it is, and as it has been. The faculty of sight invites the other senses to the table. It is, for many, an experience in translating.

A photograph is a storyteller; this one from Eisenhower's library tells many stories. I am, I know, looking at remains. Hundreds or thousands of remains. How many souls linger in this ruin? Total strangers who had no business in each other's orbits; abandoned together, incinerated. It is most macabre, and still, I stare. Aside from the brutality, which is distinctly human, the pile, too, evokes the *lack* of humanity; an absence of tale. I will imagine these people as people, for my own care, but I am forced to confront their end, their aftermath, their cremation, because I'm looking at a goddamn mountain of bones.

When you rely on oral and written testimony, there is only the storyteller.

You argue: This photograph does not tell everything. And yes, perhaps from this angle, the wretched pile obscures something sitting behind it. A barking dog; a crying baby; a rose—some sense of life. That is for the imagination to decide. It is a distraction.

But! When there are words; now your mind must grapple and configure. You must contemplate the structure, must decide what to see; you must listen for inflection; define and sit with vocabulary, all as you're trying to read. *Ah, you must be able to read.* Or, at least, you must know someone who can read in your stead.

Of utmost import: A storyteller must be alive to tell it.

This is where I place myself, staring at the pages in Polish; my cousin's Holocaust testimony.

2.

It costs a pretty penny to have Szymon's testimony translated from Polish.

At first, my order (on a freelance website) is refused.

Chatbooster39: *Hi amycook430, Is that a joke? :)*

"Chatbooster39" is not amused, despite the smile emoji, but I don't know why.

He continues, a few minutes later: "You paid $15 for 200 words. [But there are] 7 pages. I will send you a refund. Please don't order again."

That seems . . . harsh. What am I missing?

But he writes again. "I can see you are new to this platform. It's all good. I don't do handwritten documents. But the remaining 7 pages for $15, from which I will receive $12, is insulting even for a person from Bangladesh."

Oof. Does he think I'm a racist, or merely an American who relies on cheap labor? Some combination? Perhaps I am missing a subtlety, but isn't he the translator? Just tell me what I owe you! I push on, offer him more than a lot of money if he can bring me closer to my family.

He accepts the order, and I wait.

I still don't know what "even for a person from Bangladesh" was supposed to mean. Did I demean his dignity?

3.

I wrote a speculative essay in the summer of 2021, featuring this cousin Szymon, the bereft father. At the time, I knew far less. I was cribbing from a French and Hebrew form submitted to the Israel Commemorative Institute of Martyrs and Heroes in which Cousin Arthur (son of Cousin Szymon) accounts for the existence of a sibling, long dead before Arthur's own birth. In the Jewish religion, you keep someone's memory alive by going to their grave and leaving a pebble on their grave marker. For 6 million people who don't have real graves, having a historic record of their existence was the best that could be done. We keep their memories alive by knowing who they were.

In the essay, I primarily explored what it means to be the second son—especially when the first is a ghost. In my mind, and then on the page, I had assumed the long-dead child to be a little boy. Son of Szymon, big brother to Arthur, even in absentia. I wanted them, subconsciously, to wear the same face. Before and after copies.

Life offers so few surprises.

4.

When Chatbooster39's translation finally arrives, I scan through the dense paragraphs, eager for details.

"The baby was freezing, but she sensed she wasn't allowed to cry."

I slow down. *She.* Szymon never says daughter (he prefers "baby" and then "child"), but there is new evidence: she. This shadow child was a little girl. A little girl, hidden in woods and basements, brought on breast and on back to safety, again and again, diminishing though safety would come to be.

I read quickly now. When his family was later imprisoned, Szymon had been able to pay so that his toddler would be smuggled out and taken to safety, yet again.

He goes on:

"I kissed the child goodbye, and they took her with them. I was permitted to accompany them outside the prison gate. They drove by car towards Bochnia, where they lived."

This was late August 1943.

The liquidation of Bochnia began on the first of September.

Over the next six weeks, the 15,000 Jews of Bochnia were sent to Auschwitz, or killed on the spot. Including Szymon's daughter.

"My spirit had crumbled"

5.

Szymon and his family had been jailed, he says, in a town called Myślenice, Poland, over 100 kilometers from home; my mind jumbles the letters, and "mish-lay-nee-tza" reconfigures itself to be "my silence." I think about what Szymon accomplished, on that March morning in 1947, speaking his child back to life, for purposes of giving this testimony. In his memory, his child laughs and smiles; cries, sleeps, calls for her tata.

I read his words, again and again, even referring back to the thick Polish characters I cannot translate. I try to make them louder.

6.

What later became Yad Vashem, the memorial and museum dedicated to those lost in the Holocaust, was first proposed mid-Holocaust, in September 1942 by Mordechai Shenhavi, a Galician Jew who was part of the Zionist youth movement. The idea for the document he authored, "The Idea of Commemorating All Victims of the Jewish Catastrophe Caused by the Nazi Horrors and the War," first came to him in a dream.

The term *Yad Vashem* comes from the Torah:

> And I will give them, in My House, and within My walls, a monument and a name (yad vashem). Better than sons or daughters, I will give them an everlasting name which shall not perish. (Isaiah 56:5)

Yad Vashem has the statements of over 131,000 survivors. I think of the people who bore witness to just one story. On March 23, 1947, someone takes down Szymon's testimony. Later, someone catalogs it as Film Reel N-074/4. Someone writes it by hand and then someone duplicates it, using a typewriter. The recording clerk, whose name appears on the written testimony, is called "Turska H." Are all of the someones Turska H.? Someone microfilms it in the year 2000. Four years after Szymon's death.

I spend time thinking about the someones, the witnesses who did the labor of memory. Did they speak Polish, or German? Yiddish? Did they speak a language with which Szymon was completely unfamiliar, so that their words twisted like branches around the room? Were there translator "someones" focused on making sure they had it exactly right? Were they older men, or younger women; Jewish, Christian, German, French, Italian? Repatriated, expatriates, maybe American, British? Were they also survivors?

Were they, like Mordechai Shenhavi, living in the Middle East, coming back to the places from which the fire of vibrant Judaism had been virtually extinguished?

Did any of those someones have a little one at home? How lucky they were. Szymon said, of the Germans who arrested him, "One of them suggested shooting the child on the spot, while the other said it would be a waste of a bullet."

"I saw," Shenhavi recalled in 1946, "millions walking toward Zion with tombstones on their shoulders . . . and they chose a location, and each of them took down his tombstone . . . and the monument of their lives was thus erected . . . one kilometer long, one kilometer wide, and 100 meters high."

One million people visit Yad Vashem every year.

7.

Here are where my family threads are strong. Szymon was born in 1911; his wife was older by one year. He was from Sieniawa, and she from Rozwadów, 70 kilometers northwest. I know that these towns were ravaged by the First World War, and by pogrom.

"Pinie," Szymon's sister, would grow up to be my great-grandmother, Pauline. She was eight years Szymon's senior, and arrived at Ellis Island, accompanied by distant relatives, on November 26, 1920, at the age of 17.

Pauline settled in Brooklyn, and married a man who had escaped the front lines of World War I thanks to a Jewish lieutenant, who assigned him to the bakery. They raised two girls, one of whom raised my mother.

Back in Poland, Szymon's wife gave birth to their first child in 1941—the child who perished either in Bochnia or Auschwitz. After the war, Szymon and his wife settled in Wałbrzych, Poland, and then in Zurich; he would move to Paris after his wife's death. They raised two other children, Arthur and Alice.

Here are where my threads fray. Szymon and Pauline's sister, Lea, appears on a document in 1941, which translates to "Questionnaire for the measurement of the Jewish population of Krakow." Months later, a letter from a German clerk to the Nazi government bears her name, and the names of her husband and child. "These people were served with the relocation order for December 27th yesterday, on December 24th," it reads. "As I have already mentioned, I started taking over the company yesterday, so the current staff is indispensable to me. . . . For this reason, I kindly ask the above-mentioned Jews to be exempted from deportation and to be issued with identity cards."

Then: nothing. Lea and her family disappear.

Other accounts of the family name a sister, Hena, who lived from 1906 to 1944 (and her husband: "Unknown" Adler), and a brother, Leibisch, born in 1907. They, too, vanish from history. My mother, to this day, still swears that there were a dozen siblings.

Most do not appear in Szymon's translation at all.

8.

Szymon's ordeal is absurd, in the sense that it does not seem to have been possible to have survived it. This, best I can understand, is his story.

Szymon places us in 1942, when the Germans arrived in Sieniawa, where Szymon and his family had been living since the outbreak of war. There, he was forced into hard labor, clearing forests. After it became clear that innocent Jews were being killed, Szymon made preparations to escape, obtaining Aryan papers for his family. It was just at this time when they "learned that most Jews in Sieniawa would have to be relocated." Perhaps it is the translation, but the tone of this shocks me.

"Are you Jewish?" I hear in my head.

Historians place the extermination of the Jews of Sieniawa that August. Szymon's daughter, at the time, was nine months old. That same month, Szymon had been commanded to come in front of the Judenraete. He chose to hide instead, seeking shelter in a bunker he'd built in his home. He did so in fear of being robbed, only to later find out that he'd saved his own life; "All the Jews who came to the Judenraete had been killed. We saw how Gestapo agents led Jews out of their apartments and shot them on the street." He stayed in the bunker, alone, for four days.

He later found safety in Kraków, but that was short-lived. One night, he heard a knock on the door, and "a German voice [said]: "Hier wohnt ein jude" (A Jew lives here). At gunpoint, and having no money or diamonds to immediately forfeit, his family's Aryan papers were taken instead. Then, in February 1943: "Our hostess approached us before evening and informed us that she had discovered we were Jews." Running from unknown pursuers, Szymon and his young family spent the overnight hours hiding in freezing woods.

The narrative leaps from escape to escape, weeks of insecurity reduced to the space between sentences. On March 10, 1943, again, fear: "The policeman waited for my wife for half an hour and left an order for her to come to the police station the next day with the baby. My wife, of course, did not come."

June 28, 1943; the beginning of an end. Again, finding themselves shelterless ("the host told us he was afraid to keep us unregistered"), Szymon turns to an acquaintance to help them find lodging. Tadeusz Kaczmarek, a government worker, arranges for an apartment; Szymon says Kaczmarek even came to greet them. "We all ate dinner together. He shared a bed with me. My wife invited him to dinner the next day."

Instead of coming for dinner, Kaczmarek sends the Gestapo. This feels unbearable to me. What had Kaczmarek been thinking as they shared a bed; as he had been offered the kindness of room and board? The Gestapo men beat Szymon half to death in front of his child; "my wife managed to escape through the window, naked, without a child and a penny."

"They're beating daddy," the child yelled as she ran around the yard.

This is where his life splits into two. It is from this moment that Szymon is taken to prison; it is from this moment that he bribes for his child's freedom, sending her, unknowingly, to her death. It is from this moment that Szymon is sent to a labor camp called Bieżanów, and then the ghetto at Skarżysko Kamienne. It is from this moment that he escapes, ending up at a railway station, where he assaults a member of the railway police so forcefully that he finds himself the time to escape. Everything that will be comes from betrayal.

September 1943: "I went to the train station in order to get to Kraków. I was fortunate to finally be able to see my wife. We lived together from then until the Soviets arrived."

But that was 20 months later. He says nothing of the interstitial time, all of which his life must have been in danger. There is just silence. The liberation of Kraków occurred on January 18, 1945.

8.

I was born 33 years and one day after Szymon's testimony is preserved. I am raised in a Conservative Jewish synagogue; both of my grandfathers, including Pauline's son-in-law, are involved in synagogue leadership, bridging the divide for so many survivors who found their way to the United States. When the Soviet Union is dissolved, our synagogue brings over Jewish families and provides for them until they can provide for themselves. We are instructed that this is how we heal the world.

From the very start, I am a storyteller, wanting to fill the air with words and sentences, characters and plot. Passover, 1985. I am five. As we tried to find a parking spot on the salt-air streets of Brighton Beach, near my great-grandparents' apartment on Ocean Ave., I remember my mother telling me, in hushed voice, that Great-Grandma Pauline had immigrated from Poland as a girl. She'd left behind her parents and about a dozen siblings, only one of whom she ever saw again. Simon lived, exotically, in France.

The message I understood (which many of us got, when it came to our elders and the war) was to tread lightly. Don't ask questions. I was already suspicious of "old people," and this instruction did little to abate that fear. I couldn't fathom these folks, who moved with such deliberation, as having had any lives before this one, where they covered their couch in plastic.

Papa Oscar would perform the entire seder in that language they simply called Jewish. I, at five years old, would sit on the shag carpet, mesmerized by the sing-song cadence of the trope. When it came time, at the end of the meal, to find the Afikoman, my little brother and I would be dispatched with my mother's teenage cousins to retrieve it. When one of us did (most likely in a bedroom drawer, where Susie or Karen would lift us up to retrieve the missing matzah), Papa Oscar would reach into the front pocket of his old-person brown pants and pull out a quarter for each child. Put it somewhere safe, my mother would say.

Szymon tells us, of 1943:

> I was able to conceal and keep three diamond-like rings on me. I got in touch with these Jews and suggested that, after being released, they should take my child and pretend she's a Hungarian citizen. They willingly agreed to it. It was necessary to obtain the consent of the prison police. I promised one [policeman] two rings, and he undertook this task.

My great-grandparents were not wealthy. Papa Oscar was a furrier, until he was disabled by cancer. Great-Grandma Pauline kept a Jewish home. She killed and prepared her own gefilte fish in the bathroom tub. Their son-in-law paid their rent.

And, somewhere along the way, I learned about the importance of having a quarter in your pocket. And the consequences of what you might be buying.

9.

July 21, 2022. Subject line: *The Gig you ordered: "I will natively translate english to polish and polish to English" from Chatbooster39 is ready for your review.*

I was about to enjoy an afternoon run. I opened my laptop instead.

"Wulwik Szymon, on Aryan papers under the same name, born in 1911 in Siniawa, county Jarosław, merchant, lived in Katowice until the war, during the occupation in Siniawa, Kraków and camps. Currently in Wałbrzych, Biały Kamień, Traugutta 131 street."

Midway through the second page, the typeface changes abruptly from black to red. The text reads, "(A [Judenraete] was a World War II administrative agency imposed by Nazi Germany on Jewish communities across occupied Europe, principally within the Nazi ghettos.)" I fumble to understand exactly what's happening. I know what a Judenraete is already. Seven years of Hebrew school and a lifetime of being a Jew has me pretty well-prepared. Is Szymon explaining it to a someone? I look back at the original Polish and don't see the parentheses at all.

And then I figure it out. Without warning, Chatbooster39, my translator, has inserted himself into Szymon's testimony, explaining references he does not think I'll understand. Now, I'm riled up. I feel . . . invaded. On my own behalf and on Szymon's. I scroll and scroll and scroll; more red ink. Half a dozen times, Chatbooster39's definitions appear, between my cousin's words. Where there are German terms replacing the Polish, he's defined those, too, this time in blue.

I will think about this for weeks. I am simultaneously livid and a little bit amused. He thinks, perhaps he has gone the extra mile for a client. But it is not what I asked him to do. This is not what I overpaid for. Perhaps he has done this because of other feedback in the past, where people were uneducated about certain terms. Maybe they didn't have Google.

I could just delete his intrusions. Pretend that they never existed.

But then I talk myself down. I find it interesting that he doesn't mention that a Judenraete was, in fact, made of Jews. That one of the most evil parts of the Holocaust was the fact that the Nazis forced Jews to turn each other in. That, in fact, the resistance was weakened by the fact that your own neighbor could report you.

I talk myself down because now my translator, like the recording clerk "Turska H." and the countless, nameless someones, is a part of this story now, too.

As, I guess, am I, relating our story to you.

10.

The Jewish Agency for Palestine/Search Bureau published a book called the *Register of Jewish Survivors (II)*. It contains the names of 57,702 Jews who "were found in Poland after the liberation." The book's introduction goes into some detail about the curation of this list. The lack of complete data, the authors explain, is understandable even in its horror. Disclosure required survivors—who had lived through the end of the world—to identify themselves as Jewish. To put themselves back on a list.

"For the most part, however, the waning interest in the registration was due to neglect and failure to appreciate the importance of the matter."

Eisenhower's fears come true. Many deny or minimize the Holocaust; others blame the Jews for their own massacre. The state that is created to harbor the survived is demonized, and terrorized. But on page 209, in the first column of this book, is my cousin's name. His wife is unaccounted for, although she lived until 1975.

There is no record of their murdered daughter's name. On the Yad Vashem form that Cousin Arthur filled out on his sibling's behalf, 40 years after her death, he put a question mark where her name is supposed to be. Some internet records list her as Monyuche Wulwik, which I cannot make much sense of, as I try to pronounce it with the cadence my great-grandmother brought from Sieniawa; perhaps it's a transliteration of Monika, which means "wise." I don't know.

In January 2024, I obtain records from an organization called JRI-Poland. Its director, Stanley Diamond, has obtained birth records, from official Polish archives, for two dozen members of my family. Including Szymon and his siblings Lea, Hena, Leibisch, and Szymon's child, born in 1941.

A son.

Mendel.

I can't tell you I am surprised that the translation, again, has gone wrong.

Stanley Diamond's records are pretty detailed. He has done this work for decades, excavating archives so that our lines of ancestry are a little firmer than before. When he passes away, the following December, his entire organization has impossibly large shoes to fill.

Stanley has become part of my story, too. Part of Pauline's story. And Szymon's. And Lea's, and Leibisch's, and Hena's.

My youngest niece is now three years old, an age that Mendel never lived to see. Her name is Hannah. Named not intentionally after her great-great-aunt Hena, but someday, I will tell her her family's story, anyway. Hannah lives in a suburban town in New Jersey, where the local synagogue has recently been the target of spray paint and swastikas.

This summer, Hannah made a new friend at school, whose name is Marty.

She calls him, "Mawwwty" with a thick Jewish accent.

The Tamarisk Tree
Anil Classen

Junko looked up into the earnest eyes of her brother, Jun'ichi.

"You're going to end up living with our parents forever," Jun'ichi said slowly, cutting into his steak that looked a little too bloody.

Junko felt her mother's eyes on her, but she would not look up. Even if she did, her mother would carry on staring, oblivious to the way she shamed her daughter by not defending her. Junko's back remained stiff. She still had a fragment of pride left. Allowing Jun'ichi to see her confidence wobble, even for a second, was not an option.

"It's easy for you to talk," Junko said calmly. "Our parents introduced you to your wife."

Jun'ichi's chair scraped the floor like a sharp intake of breath. His eyes narrowed, blunt with anger as he stood up, legs wide apart. Junko knew she had him cornered. He had never been good with girls. Their mother had saved him the embarrassment. She ushered the idea into life, whispering into their father's ear, making it feel like it was his idea to invite an old business colleague to an impromptu lunch. From there, a dinner plan was hatched. When they saw the man again, he brought along his daughter with droopy eyes. She was also struggling to find the perfect match.

"Can't you just . . . find someone?" Jun'ichi asked, his voice raised a few octaves, signaling exasperation. Junko knew his succinct, biting words would plague her for days afterwards.

It would be easy to flip the table over, ignoring the broken plates, food flying in all directions like a hit scene in a mafia film. Her father enjoyed those types of films. He'd sit, late into the night, alone, cracking peanuts between his thumb and index finger. Instead of the bravado of those men her father admired, Junko chose placidity. She bit into the already cold pork dumpling she knew would be tasteless.

Leaving dinner disgruntled, Junko made her way to the café to meet up with Kazue, her friend and eternally optimistic matchmaker. After Kazue reported yet another successful pairing, Junko caved. There was no point battling the tide. The current of wise quips would only engulf her. The worst was yet to come, photographic evidence detailing countless matches Kazue had successfully administered like a ninja cupid. To solidify her case, she presented images of smiling couples like evidence in a court trial.

"His name is Sota," Kazue said slowly, sensing Junko would forget this important detail.

"Sota," Junko said slowly, nodding. "How do you spell that?"

Junko held a serious face for a second, enjoying Kazue's disbelief, before her laughter burst free.

"Do I look like a joke to you?" Kazue asked tersely, standing up.

"No, no. Come on. Sit. God, where did your sense of humor go?"

Kazue eyed her, gauging if the situation was worth her time before sitting down again, ironing out the back of her leather skirt before she settled into the seat again.

"He's not from Osaka, but he's in IT," Kazue continued, taking out her notebook. "He is shy, so don't ask him too many questions, okay? It's a date, not an interrogation."

"Why are you talking to me like I'm an idiot?" Junko snapped, forcing a smile after noticing Kazue's tight expression.

Junko spent a solid 20 minutes plucking her eyebrows that evening after noticing the tiny arch in Kazue's. She wanted the same effect, a look of piqued interest, of always being alert, open to any possibility. The result did not come close to Kazue's manicured brows. Junko's were too wide apart to begin with. She hated how her plump cheeks, a gift from her mother, did nothing for her except make her look permanently tired or bloated. There was still a glimmer of hope that her lips, her only saving grace, would work in her favor. While she hated their fullness, they managed to stop men on the subway, their eyes glued to the delicate indentation of her upper lip.

Standing with the bathroom cabinet door open, the shelves lined with her mother's facial products, Junko bent forward, running her hands through her hair in an attempt to loosen the strands and, most importantly, add volume. After she shot back upward toward the mirror, she paused, checking her face from various angles. Her cascading hair was pleasing. The satisfaction lasted only a moment, though, before she noticed the bubble of hair above her fringe already starting its steady deflation.

As Junko walked down an alley later in the evening, a row of red and black lanterns swaying in the distance, she thought how silly she had been. How could anyone willingly fall into the trap of being set up? She pushed the door open, the ringing bell making a few diners turn. The tiny restaurant for her date had a simple layout, a classic U-shaped table formation around a chef standing front and center with an immaculate chef's hat for added effect. The tension lessened in her chest as she realized she would not have to sit opposite her prospective love interest, putting herself on display to be gauged and prodded like a prize cow.

Junko looked at the grainy picture on her phone. It offered little detail. The hairstyle, abrupt and short, matched the man sitting at the end of the counter. He was watching the chef cut into a slab of tuna so pink, it looked like plastic.

"I am sorry I'm late. I'm Junko," she said, approaching him with her head slightly bowed.

As he turned away from the cooking prep, Junko flinched. There was something, something she couldn't quite place that stopped her breathing. It lasted only a split second before he smiled, a row of white teeth asking for a reciprocal gesture, a signal for the conversation door to be opened between them.

"I am Sota, but you already know this," he said in a deep voice, at odds with his soft baby features. His forced smile disappeared quickly. "You're not late. I'm— I'm always early."

Junko nodded before fumbling with her handbag, trying to hang it on the hook underneath the table. Looking back up, she caught him watching her intently. His eyes followed the lines of her navy-blue trench coat, the one she had eyed for months through a designer boutique window, waiting for the sale.

"You can hang your coat at the door. There's a rail."

Junko closed her eyes, realizing her childishness. She had decided to wear something totally inappropriate underneath, a plan B should the date turn into a nightmare. Her black halter neck was cut low, to drive off any conservative admirer. Her risqué choice would also shock a man-about-town into a well of countless questions he would busy himself with instead of noticing her excuse to use the bathroom and never returning.

"I'm fine. I'm always cold," Junko said hurriedly.

She realized too late how this could come across, how her reaction could be seen as standoffish. It was easier not looking up from her woven placemat than into an expression of disappointment.

"I'll be right back," he said as he stood up, bumping into a waitress, who smiled quickly before her lips returned to a frozen line of irritation.

"Where—"

"The bathroom," he answered with a smile. It was meant to placate, but only made Junko look at him even more intently.

"Shall I order you something?" she asked, flipping the menu open.

"Green tea, please."

Normally this would have elicited a laugh from Junko, followed by some or other smart quip about the nonexistent alcohol in tea. Her lips remained sealed, though. The loud thud of metal hitting hard plastic made her look at the cooking station. The chef had just sliced through a batch of enoki mushrooms, creating two perfect halves before searing them in shallow butter. Tilting her face to one side, she inhaled the nuttiness of the browning butter. A nagging thought would not let go of her. A question rolled around in her head like a restless marble.

Why was he so familiar?

When Sota returned, they watched the chef prepare an order for the couple next to them, a slim platter of finely sliced sashimi that gleamed under the overhead lighting. Junko nodded as Sota smiled at her before sipping his tea, neither of them quite knowing how to bridge the dividing silence opening itself like a wide expanse of water, smooth as quicksilver.

"You're a lot prettier than Kazue said."

She nodded at the compliment, the periscope of her shyness quickly surveying the area, to see if it was safe to let its guard down. Junko noticed the tiny cut on his chin. Was it a sign of clumsiness? Or an effort to look groomed? How would he look with more facial hair? His profile was angular, so a beard would add an edge to his softer features. He could have modeled for a high-end campaign. His jutting cheekbones and jawline could have been shaped by any makeup artist until his face took on a steely robotic appearance.

Junko's mind would not stop racing. The feeling of recognition lingered. It tapped against the glass window of memory like a woodpecker intent on being heard.

"How do you know Kazue?" she finally asked, after people started talking around them, making their lack of conversation even more apparent.

"We were in the same company last year before she changed jobs. Now she's a highflyer," he said with a small smile before he shrugged his shoulders, sending his white shirt into concertina folds.

"Yes. She's going to accomplish great things."

"And you?" he asked, both eyebrows raised in anticipation.

"Me? Ah, I know her from a dance class we took together. She's so talented . . . actually makes me a bit jealous."

He nodded a little too enthusiastically. Junko suddenly wished she had placed her food order sooner.

Their shared awkwardness was beginning to drag her spirits down.

A waitress walked up to them, this time a different one, a girl around their age with a severe fringe grazing her eyebrows. Her bored expression spoke volumes behind pinched lips. With pen in hand, she waited irritably for their order.

"The beef udon, please," Junko said before looking at Sota, whose finger was running down the list on his menu.

"For me . . . err . . . the . . . nikujaga."

"Anything else?" the waitress asked without looking up from her pad.

"Maybe some yakimochi? I haven't had it in a while," Sota said.

A sudden smile lifted his face dramatically.

"Fine," the waitress said before flitting through the side door beside the cooking station.

"You enjoy yakimochi?"

Junko nodded. The rice cakes were a treat her mother always prepared in winter. Junko loved the caramelized scent from the frying pan. It always made their home feel cozy against the dropping temperature outside.

"Do you enjoy it?" she asked slowly.

"It's one of my favorites."

They nodded, looking in opposite directions as the traffic swayed back and forth in front of the large window running the length of the restaurant. Just as she was about to call the waitress to ask about their order, the yakimochi arrived, four rectangular rice blocks puffing themselves aggressively upward. Sota pushed the plate toward Junko, nudging her with a shake of his head. As he poured soya sauce into a tiny bowl, she watched him smile, a set of dimples appearing, dented by magic into his cheeks. And then the realization hit her. The vacuum of memory sliced the moment in half. Recognition ripped her from the restaurant table with meaty hands, pressing her arms roughly with intent.

"Junko? Are you alright?"

She looked up into concerned eyes, a set belonging to a stranger before. Now his eyes were familiar.

"You haven't touched your food," he said in between chewing.

Junko looked down at her plate before her eyes swung back up toward him. His eyes were closed in silent appreciation. A sense of pity swelled inside her. Suddenly, it was painfully clear who he was, only she wondered how he could have forgotten her. Or was this a game? They had not seen each other for over ten years.

"Are you from Osaka?" Junko asked, before biting into her cake, regretting her mistake instantly. She had forgotten to dip it in the sauce bowl.

"No."

"So, where are you from?"

"Tokyo, originally."

"Hmm. Then you came here after college?"

"Yes. It's been two years now," he answered, not looking at her.

Junko felt the temperature shift slightly. She noticed his jaw tighten, but she couldn't tell if it was from his chewing or nerves.

"I feel like we've . . . met," she said slowly.

He stopped chewing.

"No, I've never seen you before today."

Junko's eyes fell on his lap, noticing the clenched fist. Sota quickly pulled his hand beneath the table, a red flourish of embarrassment moving across his cheeks. Her instinct told her to leave. All it would take were a few easy strides. She still had her coat on. Her bag could be unhooked in one movement like a pickpocket. She didn't even have to turn around and look at him one last time. Kazue would be satisfied with a little lie. She'd roll her eyes at the missed opportunity, the date not leading to more like a series of matryoshka dolls eliciting wonder with each new painted face appearing. Junko remained in her seat, though. She watched the waitress take her plate away, quickly replacing it with another.

"We don't have to do this," Junko finally said, once their meal had been delivered, followed by a curious look from the waitress. She was clearly used to more conversation.

"What?" he asked, his head down as he looked at their food.

"We don't have to pretend. I won't tell anyone I saw you."

"I'm not sure—"

"Riku, I—"

"Who's Riku? My name is Sota."

The clenched jaw was back, only this time his eyes shifted nervously. Junko hated cornering him this way. Making anyone feel uncomfortable was so far from her normal nature. She always felt like a bully when insisting on the truth, something her mother always said was overrated, like the truth ever brought any real joy, she would say with a bitter laugh.

"You've changed your hairstyle," Junko said before taking a sip of her wine, her only consolation for such a difficult date. "And you've lost a lot of weight."

She remembered how his long hair brushed his ears playfully as he huffed behind his classmates, chasing an elusive football across the field in front of his apartment building. His fringe had the habit of falling into his eyes. He'd constantly sweep an irritated hand across his forehead in intervals like a windshield wiper detecting the first drops of rain.

"All I wanted was to meet someone," he said slowly, deliberately.

"What?"

"I just—" he said, stopping as his eyes closed. "I just wanted to meet someone."

Junko looked down at her still untouched noodles. She knew in a few minutes, the sauce would harden if she didn't move a chopstick through them.

"Someone to have a meal with," he continued, "maybe even start spending time together, see where it could lead to."

Junko looked up as his chopsticks hit the plate. His head fell into his hands.

"And of all people, Kazue matches us together," he said, laughing lightly from behind fingers blocking his face. There was no depth to the laughter, though.

"I—"

"You've changed your hair as well, Junko."

"I have, thank goodness," she said with a nervous laugh.

"You outgrew your tomboy phase. I didn't recognize you when you walked in. We've both changed, haven't we?"

"Only I kept my name, Riku."

"Don't call me that. That's not my name."

"And Sota is?"

He looked at her with the saddest eyes before he stood up, looking down at the untouched food. The waste would no doubt make the chef question his cooking skills. Regret lined Riku's face mercilessly. It took a chisel to his cheeks, dragging the soft lines down. He suddenly looked older as he pulled a dark blue scarf around his neck roughly.

"Just forget about this . . . about this chance meeting. Please . . ."

"What?"

"Please don't tell anyone you saw me."

He was so quick in turning, Junko couldn't answer. He pulled his windbreaker from a hook and walked out. Junko caught the shock in the waitress's face before she idiotically forced a smile, fishing out her purse to pay as more rain washed up against the restaurant window.

The bad weather gave the city a reprieve, even if only momentarily, Junko thought as she finally unhooked her bag. Outside, the streets, normally lined with commuters, were quiet, streetlights lifting up the downpour in confetti streams. Cars and motorcycles forced their way through heavy puddles running in all directions, creating an uneven boomerang of sound. On the way to her bus stop, Junko lit a cigarette, watching the steam rising from the pavement, wrapping the street in a sheath of cloud, neon signage peeking through only slightly. Rough edges of supermarkets and pharmacies were visible, park bench legs disappearing into the night, giving the illusion that everything was floating, elevated above wet paving. Junko inhaled strongly, the smoke filtering its way into her mouth. The delicious swirl of nicotine confirmed why the bad habit stuck. The timetable above her head announced a long wait. Calling a taxi felt tiresome. The bus ride home was more enjoyable anyway. She always fell asleep easily as the bus engine vibrated metal against rubber, humming a rhythm into the journey, an odd lullaby, but one that was effective in its simplicity.

Riku filtered into her mind. His distressed face resurfaced, echoing a tight feeling in her stomach. A shame hit her solidly between the eyes like the start of a migraine. She hated how her need to understand things outweighed the embarrassment she had caused him. Junko was so wrapped up in her thoughts, she didn't notice being pushed slightly along the bench by someone waiting for the bus.

"When I saw your picture, I thought for a moment, is it you? But I didn't think it possible. What were the odds, right?"

Junko didn't turn at the sound of his voice. Any sudden movements could have scared him off. All it would take was her turning too quickly and he'd disappear into the street, under the camouflage of rain and busy traffic. If anything bad happened now, she could tell herself later it was nothing more than a daydream, a moment she had hoped for. In the end, the evening was nothing more than fantasy.

"Maybe part of me wanted you to recognize me, to feel seen again, even after all this time," Riku said, facing her.

"Why did you agree to the date if you suspected it was me? I don't understand."

"Neither do I."

"Your parents went crazy when you disappeared."

Johatsu. Before Riku went missing, this was just a word, often heard in hushed conversation, three syllables creating the fear that forced children to be quiet, like anticipating the bogeyman. Johatsu. Even saying it out loud felt like you were casting a spell. But it wasn't folklore. It wasn't a fable even. It existed beneath the veneer of all communities, people willingly leaving the world they lived in to start over, to forget, to run from what had caused unhappiness.

"You could have spoken to someone, instead of . . ." Junko whispered.

"What?"

"Cutting ties and just vanishing. It wasn't fair," she said a little louder, still not daring to look at him until he sighed.

Junko turned her head ever so slowly. The pull was too much to ignore. He looked straight ahead at the moving cars creating elongated beams of white and red light as they sped through the water-slicked street.

"You don't understand. It was all my fault," he said, fingers now over his eyes. A car blasted a hooter loudly before swerving. "I should have noticed the signs. Reina was in over her head."

Junko saw a flash of his sister, a goofy smile lighting up her face, hair parted in the middle so that it hung elegantly along her cheeks.

"No one saw what was happening," Junko said slowly.

"But I did. I saw her sinking in all that faith, the faith my parents were convinced was more important than . . ."

"Than what?"

"Than being good parents, I suppose."

The rain started to pelt down harder. The puddle on the pavement quivered under the weight of each new droplet, ripples moving from the epicenter in determined circles.

"Reina, she tried," he said after a loud sniff. "I see that now. I remember everything. How she tried to be the perfect daughter, the perfect church member, giving up her weekends to knock on doors she knew would be slammed in her face before she had even finished her first sentence."

"What happened wasn't anyone's fault."

"You're wrong."

It was painful to see him shake his head. Junko watched him lace his fingers together. For a horrified second, she thought he would start praying.

"Do you know that we never had birthdays?"

"Yes. She told me."

"Reina never blew out candles on a cake. I was the older brother. I never thought, not for a second, how important it was. She was probably dreaming of a normal birthday. Hell, I was dreaming about it. Why didn't I think she was doing the same?"

Junko was grateful for the solitude of the bus stop, the weather making waiting inhospitable, fate allowing a rare moment of privacy in a city constantly in movement, always alive with sound, people rushing toward a destination, jostling for coveted space.

"You know it was me," Junko said after she finally made up her mind.

"Huh?"

"I found her."

"Found her?"

"I was late at school that day, clearing up after the drama club rehearsal. We were doing *Hamlet*. Everyone was so excited. I . . ."

The moment returned like all flashbulb moments, alive and static in their clarity. The passing years had done nothing to color the memory of Reina's ashen face. Junko's parents had lied. They had told her time would erase the bad, those images that haunted, that robbed her of sleep. They promised only the good would remain like water and soil giving way to gold. The truth had slammed a flat-palmed hand on top of Junko's wish to forget.

"I ran at the first opportunity," Riku said, wiping his nose roughly. "I had saved up enough. I didn't even stay for the funeral. What a shitty thing to do. All I left was a letter, and not a good one at that."

"Are you still running?"

Riku patted her thigh lightly before he stood up, zipping his jacket all the way to his chin, not that this small protection was anything against the deluge of water now running over the curved plastic of the bus shelter. Junko wanted to tell him to wait, to sit it out with her, maybe even accompany her home, but his eyes were too wet to allow kindness in. They spoke only of a blinding sense of loss no one could ever wipe clear.

"You know you can stop running whenever you're ready," Junko whispered, taking his hand suddenly.

He looked down at their hands, the connection feeling forced somehow.

"I know. It just feels . . ."

"Easier?"

Riku tried to smile, his lips moving upward and then stopping. His left eye closed in a slight wink. Junko thought she imagined it, but a nod of the head told her otherwise.

"I jog on the weekends," Junko said as she pulled her hair into a ponytail.

A bus turned the corner, heading toward them.

"Jog?" Riku asked, clearly surprised.

"Yes. It's *my* form of running."

The bus door slammed open. Junko stepped onto the first metal step. The conductor eyed her suspiciously with bloodshot eyes before giving Riku a withering look.

"Maybe you can join me?" she asked, tilting her head to one side.

"Maybe. I have your number."

As the bus drove off, Riku was still at the curb, watching her with a raised hand. Junko wasn't sure if it was a farewell at all.

Both the Author and the Protagonist

Surya Maroju

I used to think I was just . . . less.

Less talented than my classmates.
Less charming than my friends.
Less worthy than anyone I met.

I wore my inferiority like a uniform—invisible maybe, but unmistakable to those who knew how to look. And the world seemed to agree with my quiet verdict: overlooked for promotions, forgotten at parties, ignored in conversations.

Neville Goddard's work appeared to me during one of my many online escapades. "Assume the feeling of the wish fulfilled," I read, as if it were as simple as changing a coat. I scoffed. My wish was to be enough—and you can't just pretend that.

But when you're tired of being invisible, even impossible things start to sound worth trying.

So I began a strange experiment. Each night, I wrote in a battered notebook—not about my day, but about the day I wished I'd had.

"Today, I was sought out for my ideas."
"Today, I walked into the room knowing I belonged."
"Today, I was seen, heard, valued."

At first, my hand shook as I wrote. The sentences felt foreign, almost dishonest. But Neville had said the outer world was only the shadow of the inner—so I kept going, making the scenes vivid, touching the feelings they gave me.

Something shifted. Not overnight, but subtly. My coworkers began asking for my input before meetings. A friend introduced me as "the most insightful person I know." One afternoon, a stranger said, "You have a presence about you," and I almost laughed out loud.

The gap between who I'd been and who I was becoming grew wider. And then one night, as I wrote, the words flowed out like they weren't mine at all:

"I am the author of my worth."

I stopped. Stared. And realized it was true. I had been writing myself into a new reality—one where I was not less than anyone, because I was no longer measuring myself against anyone.

That night, I closed the notebook. The script was finished. And when I woke the next morning, the world looked at me differently. Or maybe, finally, I looked at it the way I'd written it to be. I had become both the sculptor and the sculpture, the author and the protagonist of my world.

Under a Purple Sky
Morgan Smith

"They transferred Jason to the minimum-security prison in Walsenburg," Roberts said to his son, Ty. It was New Year's morning and the wind rocked the car as the two of them neared the summit of Loveland Pass where they would park and begin the climb of Mount Sniktau and its long, windswept ridges.

"Are you going to visit him?" Ty answered in his mocking voice.

Am I going to visit him? Roberts thought. Of course, I am, he wanted to say. He pictured himself driving south from Denver the 160 miles to Walsenburg, without his wife, Silvia, his heart pounding, as close to tears as he had been at Jason's sentencing hearing in the Denver District Court, ready to be mocked by his huge, angry youngest son but also ready to change.

"Jason thought that you were a magician, Dad. That you could just walk into that courtroom and get him probation."

Roberts shook his head. "I'm just a lawyer, Ty. More like a plumber than a magician. You fix the leak but how much water has already escaped?"

Ty made a grunting noise and turned away sharply. Roberts gripped the steering wheel and tried to focus on the steep, winding highway as they curved upward from the snow-clogged valley toward timberline and the top of the pass. The sky overhead was a pale, frigid blue, but Roberts noticed how it turned into an ominous purple along the horizon and over the surrounding mountains. A storm was coming.

"I'm going to write Jason a letter first. I'll do it as soon as we get home. Then I'll visit."

"Write him about what?"

"You'll see. I'm going to do one for you too."

Ty snorted.

"It's a new year. I'm going to change. I'll be writing it out for you after we do this climb."

"Writing it out. Another of your plans. Writing out a new reality for the old trial lawyer." Ty snorted again.

"You know, yellow is the best color for climbing." Roberts suddenly changed the subject in an effort to re-engage Ty. "You can always spot it, unlike red or something darker."

"The Aconcagua story. I've heard it before, Dad. You climbed Aconcagua in Argentina and passed a dead man wearing a yellow parka. So what?"

Roberts just gripped the steering wheel.

"The bottom line is that Jason's in prison, Dad. Three fucking years! And Mom's going to have to go into a nursing home."

"I've done my best," Roberts continued, almost whispering.

"It wasn't good enough." Ty's voice rose. "And now you want to change everything by writing us some letters. Let's drop it and just climb this damn mountain."

With Ty, Roberts thought, it was like cross-examining a witness, shifting from subject to subject, hoping to find a way to penetrate that barrier of hostility. He had thought that climbing this mountain would help, a shared victory over the brutal winds above them. Maybe it would also wipe away temporarily the thought of Jason waking up on New Year's Day in prison in southern Colorado. For all the dozens of times he, Roberts, had visited clients in prisons in almost 50 years as a lawyer, he had no idea what the inmates would do on a New Year's Day. A special meal? The usual heaps of starchy mashed potatoes? Football games on TV?

"Shit!" Ty said, pointing out the car window as Roberts parked.

"What?"

"Look!"

During the Christmas storm the wind had swept the snow off the upper ridges and blown it down into the valley. Now it was bringing it back up in gusts that swirled above them like little tornadoes. Climbing the ridge would be like being in a blizzard, except that it would be coming from below them.

"It's going to be vicious," Ty said, standing outside the car now, slowly adjusting the hood on his down parka, as if he were waiting for him, Roberts, to call the climb off. Roberts watched him for a moment, then put on his anorak. It was the New Year, time not only for a physical challenge but also for a new reality. The climb came first, however. It was going to be more intense than he had anticipated, but he couldn't turn back.

Ty took the lead. It was almost 12,000 feet here at the top of the pass and breathing was difficult. Roberts used climbing poles to give himself better balance. When he looked up, Ty was already ten yards ahead, head down, moving steadily upward. Ty's dog was trotting along next to him, a black lab undaunted by the weather. Her name was Pepper and she had belonged to Jason.

Roberts thought of all the mountains he and Ty had climbed together. Most of the 14,000-foot peaks here in Colorado, the volcanoes in Mexico, a 20,000-foot peak in Bolivia. But then it had just fizzled out. He would suggest a climb, but Ty would always have other commitments. This was the first time they had been together in at least five years.

Usually they ascended silently, each in his own world. But on the descents, Ty would open up and the Ty that Roberts remembered as a teenager would emerge, laughing, open, full of ideas and stories. It seemed bizarre to have to go through all the effort of climbing a mountain just for those few minutes of closeness on the descent, but Roberts missed that so much. Finally, he had persuaded Ty to do this New Year's Day climb with him, hoping for some reconnection.

Ty had been a steady, strong climber, reliable, prepared. At one time, Roberts had trusted him more than anyone else he climbed with—more than his more experienced friends who were often too driven to get to the summit. Or the reckless Jason.

Ahead of him, Ty moved slowly, hunched into the wind. Pepper seemed to be doing fine. As Roberts followed, watching his footing, he thought back to Aconcagua years earlier. On summit day, he and his climbing partner, Marco, were at about 21,000 feet when they saw a yellow spot in the snow high above them. As they got closer, they saw that it was a man in a yellow parka.

"Why is he waiting for us?" Marco had asked.

Roberts knew the answer but didn't say anything.

"Holy shit! It's a fucking corpse," Marco shouted when they finally reached the man.

Yes, it was a dead man in a yellow parka, sitting frozen in the snow, the sun reflecting off his iced-over face. Roberts assumed that because he was sitting, he had probably collapsed while descending. He remembered how he and Marco had laughed and laughed. Shock at finding the body? Relief that they were still alive and near the summit? Or just the giddiness of the altitude? But the man had died doing what he loved; not many people are that lucky, Roberts thought.

Looking down at the ground and watching his footing, all he could see was the wind-scoured earth, stony remnants of the path that climbers followed in summertime, little clusters of tiny dead flowers poking up out of the slabs of snow. He climbed carefully; his balance wasn't what it had once been. He didn't want to stumble, break the rhythm of his slow but relentless pace. Keeping up with Ty—or at least not falling too far back and embarrassing himself—was critical.

The wind was making a deep, moaning sound as if the whole earth were vibrating. The hood of his anorak protected his face; he would be warm enough as long as he kept moving. It was stopping that was dangerous—stopping and feeling the wind just suck the heat out of your body. This climb was an easy stroll in summer but on a winter day like this, it could be lethal.

"Dad."

The voice came from behind him. Startled, he stopped and turned. How had he gotten ahead of Ty? The wind was whipping the snow across Ty's legs so that Roberts could only see him from the knees up. They huddled close together.

"I've had it. I'm going back," Ty whispered. His face was turned away from Roberts.

"Sick?"

"No, I just don't feel like going on. You should go back too."

Stunned, Roberts shook his head, trying to catch his breath. Yes, at his age, he should be the one turning back, not Ty. But that wasn't going to happen. The most draining part of the climb was behind them; for the first time that morning, he knew that he could make the summit. Twisting away from Ty, he shook his head. You could turn back because of an injury or sickness or some objective danger like lightning but not because you just didn't feel like going on. How could Ty, in his late forties, not understand that?

Then he thought back to Jason's sentencing hearing in the District Court. Even though Jason had his own lawyer, a young woman named Petra Jacobs who knew the Denver court system intimately, Roberts understood that he had to be there, that he had to speak up for his son.

He went alone. No Ty. No Silvia. It would have been too confusing for her. But what are you, he thought, if you can't stand with your family in the most painful times? He had asked to be allowed to say a word on Jason's behalf, hoping that the judge would knock some time off the four-year sentence that Petra had negotiated with the Assistant District Attorney. A bone for all his years trying cases in these courtrooms, a bone for a shaky old man who had appeared on behalf of hundreds of defendants but never a relative, a son.

The judge, a striking-looking Hispanic woman who was probably Jason's age—early forties—stared impassively at him as he struggled to speak. He didn't know her, had never appeared in her court, yet, without any explanation, she reduced Jason's sentence to three years instead of the negotiated four. Yes, she threw him a bone but a year was a year. Ty was right, however; Jason still had three years to deal with. And Roberts still had to stand there, trembling, near tears. As the sheriff's deputies led the cursing Jason away in leg irons, Roberts knew his days as a courtroom lawyer were over.

"You sure? We've done the steepest part," he said to Ty.

Roberts wanted to see Ty's eyes, but his face was almost completely hidden by the hood of his down parka and his dark glasses. He reached out to him but Ty turned away. They stood silently with the snow swirling up around their legs. Roberts began to feel the heat draining out of his body. It was time to get moving again.

"Can you get back to the car OK?" Roberts asked finally, trying to keep his voice steady.

"Of course."

To Roberts, watching Ty turn back—giving up, in effect—was like having a dagger driven into him, but he just whispered, "Go back. Get warm. But I'm going on." Then the wind suddenly drove him to his knees.

"Dad, you're 75 years old!"

Roberts steadied himself with the climbing poles, gave Ty the car keys, and began climbing again. He started up another short steep section, picking his way carefully through the boulders. A fall here, a twisted ankle . . . In this weather, hypothermia would set in within minutes.

Then a noise. Pepper raced past. Roberts turned and saw Ty maybe a hundred yards back. He had decided to continue. Elated, Roberts waved and then continued his steady pace. He crossed over the top of a false summit and descended into the second, deeper saddle where the wind intensified again. Then, kicking steps in the hard-packed snow, he started up the narrow, final ridge to the summit. To his right, a snow slope dropped off hundreds of feet into a barren, treeless valley with a shining frozen lake in the center. Families would set up tents there in the summer, cool their feet in the frigid water, laugh, cook their meals, lay out their sleeping bags. As he and Silvia had done so many times with Ty and Jason when they were small. Now the valley was empty and forbidding.

High above, the pale sky was streaked with gathering clouds. Along the skyline, however, it was still the deep purple of a bruise. He would try to describe it to Silvia when he got home. He would try to make her see that he had found a moment of beauty.

She had started to cry when he said he was going to do this climb. What had she been trying to say? That the weather would be too harsh? That Ty wasn't ready for reconciliation? Or that he, Roberts was just too old? When he got home, she would probably still be in her bathrobe, sitting silently in the kitchen as if waiting for him to make the coffee. The nurse, a cheerful woman from Ghana, would be sitting with her. She was slipping away from him as Jason and Ty had. Could he get them back before it was too late? He told Ty that he had a plan, a change, a new direction away from the obsession of his law practice and he would write it out, but what would he say? Yet it seemed like a miracle that Ty was with him once again. He paced himself so that they would reach the summit in unison.

"Jesus, Dad!" Ty said as he slumped on the summit.

"Nasty, eh?" Roberts mumbled. "But we did it." His face seemed frozen from the wind, and he could barely speak. They were huddled behind a rock wall that earlier climbers had built.

"Got food?" Ty asked.

"I always bring something."

"That's Dad. Always prepared. The man with the peanut butter and honey sandwiches."

The scornful tone again, he thought. Calming himself, he reached in his pack for the bag with sandwiches, the roll of salami, and the chunk of cheese, but all he could find were two Milky Ways. Maybe he had left the bag at home or in the car. Silently cursing, he handed one Milky Way to Ty, who tore the wrapper off and took a huge bite.

"A Milky Way was the first candy bar I ever bought. I was eight years old, and it cost a nickel."

"You're doing a lot of reminiscing," Ty said as he took another huge bite.

"Believe it or not, my memories are mostly happy ones."

"Memories of what?" Ty's head was down. He was rubbing the lab's shoulders.

Roberts picked his words carefully. "Of being able to buy my first Milky Way over more than 60 years ago. Of having been married to your mom for 45 years. Of climbs with you. Family times. Of having been a lawyer and being able to help people."

"And Jason?" Ty interrupted.

Roberts bent over. For a few seconds, he couldn't breathe. Then he looked down the other side of the mountain, down to the New Year's Day traffic on I-70, the interstate highway way below them that led to the Vail and Copper Mountain ski areas. Skiers. Snowboarders. Families laughing together, headed for a day of fun in the Colorado mountains. Once that had been him and Silvia with Ty and Jason horsing around in the back seat.

"I tried. I was there. I stood up for him."

"What can be different now? What are you going to say in these letters? You were always there for Jason." Ty's voice rose. "You enabled him." He threw the crumpled candy wrapping at Roberts's feet. "What about the rest of us? Yes, I hate to see him in prison, but he sucked the life out of our family with his arrests, his drunkenness. You were always there to pick him up and all you got was his anger in return."

Roberts stuffed the wrapping in his pack, broke off a corner of the second Milky Way for himself, and tossed the rest to Ty. His hand was shaking.

"Ty, you don't let a family member go into a courtroom alone. You stand with him."

"A fuck of a lot of good it did."

"The judge knocked a year off his sentence," he answered weakly.

"A year out of respect for Wayne Roberts, the old bull moose trial lawyer." He snorted. "And what now? You really think Jason wants you to visit him?"

"It's the New Year, Ty. I thought—"

"The New Year. A new chance? Is that why you dragged me up here?"

"When you're 75 like me, you don't see many more good years. That's why I want to try something different."

Ty snorted. "The letters."

"Ty, my father had a heart attack when he was only 72. I'm too old to be wasting time."

They sat quietly in the pale January sunlight. Far below, the traffic made a distant rumbling sound.

"When I was a kid, there was no Eisenhower Tunnel. We had to cross Loveland Pass to get from our ranch in White Oaks to Denver. Just to see the dentist or get new eyeglasses."

Back then, stopping to climb a mountain would have seemed just an indulgence, Roberts thought. Maybe that was what most climbing was anyway. Self-indulgence. But this one was essential. He didn't know why, but he couldn't have turned back.

Ty sat on the rocks across from Roberts, holding Pepper. He was perhaps 25 pounds heavier than Roberts, powerful looking. Roberts remembered when his head would be framed with wild-looking curls. Now he was losing the hair on top. Soon the only thing they might have in common was baldness.

"In the summer, there'd be dozens of people up here." Again, like a cross examination, Roberts searched for the right topic, something that could get them on track.

"A summer stroll," Ty answered. "But that's not what you wanted, is it? You wanted this miserable wind, this . . ."

"And you? What did you want?"

Ty looked away. Roberts waited quietly for him to answer. Then he checked the tiny thermometer attached to the zipper of his anorak. "Eighteen degrees. Yet, without the wind, it feels like summer."

"Dad, I have no fucking idea why I'm here, why I agreed to this climb." The lab was gobbling up the dog treats Ty had brought. Roberts was so hungry that he thought of trying one himself.

"Dad!"

Roberts looked up, expectant. Maybe they could talk now. But Ty was standing and putting his pack on. "Jason may be in prison, but he's also free from you." Then he turned and started toward the ridge.

"Hey! Wait."

"No. I'm done. I'm going down." Then he stopped, his arms uplifted with his climbing poles pointed at Roberts. He shook them, almost like a stabbing motion and shouted something more. But his scarf was wrapped around his face and Roberts couldn't make out his muffled words.

As Ty crossed over the summit block and disappeared out of sight, Roberts pushed himself carefully to his feet, staggering slightly. Stiff from sitting, he would have fallen without the climbing poles. He began descending, bracing himself against the sudden, thumping waves of wind. He was too shaky to go back down the snow of the narrow ridge; if he fell, his body would go rocketing all the way down to the shining frozen lake. So, he descended through a jumble of boulders, his arms flailing as he tried to keep his balance. Ty was beyond him, just a dark blur in the driving snow that the swirling wind brought up from the valley. Above them, the sky seemed an even deeper purple. Hurrying, he caught up to Ty just before the short steep ascent back to the false summit.

"Ty, we need to stick together."

"This whole thing was a dumb idea," Ty shouted.

Roberts wanted to shout back at him. *What is wrong with you? This is important. To struggle. To be together.* Instead, he turned away quickly, not wanting Ty to see the pain in his face. The wind hummed against the hood of his anorak as he continued up the steep slope to the false summit, gasping, his mouth open, his leg muscles burning from the effort. He kept peeking over toward Ty, even though that meant exposing his face to the biting wind. If Ty fell and got hurt or wandered off too far to the right, it would be disastrous. There was no margin for error in this weather.

They reached the false summit, picked their way down through the rocks on its southwest side, and crossed the long saddle that led to the last ridge. Always in the past, the wind had died out on this ridge. Perhaps this was where their conversation would begin, as it had so often years ago. This was the moment Roberts had been waiting for, the payoff for the struggle to the summit. He wanted to tell Ty something about this new year and his plans but now he didn't know what. He wanted to write Jason but what about? He wanted to find something that would help him hold on to what remained of his family, but he couldn't figure out what that would be. He wanted Ty to help him.

Then suddenly he felt like he was winding down. His legs seemed to have lost their strength; he could barely move them. He turned; maybe Ty could carry his pack. But no one was there. Then Ty came into view, at least a hundred yards below him. He was running down toward the car.

"Slow down!" Roberts tried to yell as he staggered and fell backward, knowing that Ty wouldn't be able to hear him. This strange wind had lifted the snow out of the valley and deposited it on this last ridge. It had been barren when they ascended earlier, but now it was thick with the windblown snow. He lay on his back, knowing that if he lay here for long, he would be buried, his face covered with ice like the poor fucker on Aconcagua.

He thought of the visit he wanted to make to Jason, of driving to tiny Walsenburg where the prison was located, staying in a dumpy motel, visiting him in the evening after the long drive and maybe again the following morning. Could he bring him anything? Then he thought of Silvia, sitting silently by the kitchen window. Was she waiting for him to return? Somehow, despite her advancing dementia, she had known this climb was a bad idea, a desperate plan. He thought of Ty jumping in his car and turning the engine to warm up. He thought of the beautiful lab, Pepper. Maybe it would turn away from the car and start up the ridge toward him, just as it had decided to come after him earlier.

The roar of the wind was gone now and the mountain was silent. High above him, the winter sky had turned completely purple. He closed his eyes as the snow settled on his face.

Funerary Fun
Richard Stokes

At first, I thought I had stumbled
into the wrong funeral service.

The man of God was at a loss for words,
muttering tautologies passing for eulogies.

"Give the man some respect," I shouted.
"Can the phony eulogy
and give us the triple x biography.
I know the man. He wore his warts
like a badge of honor."

At the top of my lungs, I cried,
"He was despicable,
and no amount of lipstick
can make that pig respectable."

My cries fell upon
deaf ears it appears,
for no one moved.

The funeral was a travesty—
there were no friends or family,
only a few strangers
who strayed in
and stayed in
for the free-will potluck.

But no,
       I was in the right place:
       a passerby with hands folded piously,
       eyes closed prayerfully,

       laid out like an empty suit.

Writing My Way Out
Brad G. Philbrick

I. The Cage of the Given Life

I was born on a Saturday night in Moorhead, Minnesota, around 7:30 p.m.—the precise hour *The Lawrence Welk Show* aired on TV. My mother often reminded me of this as a kind of joke: "I missed Lawrence Welk that week because of you." But even as a child, I heard the subtext. I had interrupted her world. I was a disruption. That was the tone of my childhood—one of gentle reprimands wrapped in sweetness, and sharp commands cloaked in care.

From as early as I can remember, life in Moorhead felt like something I hadn't chosen. It was cold—inside and out. The winters were harsh, yes, but so was the air in our home: stiff, watchful, filled with rules and silent expectations. My mother orchestrated everything with exacting control: the way napkins were folded, how we poured milk, the volume of our voices, the posture of our ambitions. My father, a man of few words but quick temper, mainly seemed to enforce her moods. I learned early to smile, to be agreeable, to avoid becoming a problem.

I wasn't the son who earned praise or admiration. I was simply the one who didn't cause trouble. When my brothers misbehaved, I was ignored. But if I showed weakness, or if I lagged in skill or behavior—even compared to Dean, who was eight years younger—it was pointed out. Neal, two years younger than me, had a bedroom to himself. I shared a full-sized bed with Dean, not even afforded a separate bed of my own. Neal was brash, explosive, demanding—so he got his way. I was quiet, compliant, ever striving for peace. And for that, I earned nothing but erasure. No privacy, no recognition, no space of my own. Just a role to play: the good one, the accommodating one. Harmony at my expense.

By the time I was 10 or 11, I had begun keeping a journal. At first, I called it a "record book." I listed what I ate for breakfast, how many pages I read, and the temperature outside. Eventually, those lists became sentences, then stories, and finally something closer to the truth. I started to write about my mother's mood swings, my father's rants, and my brother's teasing. My little brother Dean was the spy, the informant of my behavior and actions. I wrote about how I felt when no one was looking. The pages became my only safe place.

I didn't know it then, but I was already writing a new life—one in which I had a voice.

It was in those pages that the dream began: to become a pharmacist, live on my own, and move far, far away. Pharmacy wasn't just a career idea—it was an escape plan. A way to prove I was competent, worthy, responsible, and self-sufficient. My mother wanted us boys close to home, tethered to her influence. I needed distance. I set a goal: 500 miles minimum. Indianapolis, at nearly 900 miles, would later become my triumph.

But at 13, I was still stuck in that house, watching my dreams pour out in loops of cursive across wide-ruled pages. I imagined what it would be like to wake up in a place where no one knew me, where I could arrange the kitchen the way I wanted, where I could eat what I liked without ridicule. My mother monitored even our food preferences. If I liked something she disapproved of, she'd frown and say, "That's a waste of money," or worse, "You always want the fancy things, don't you?" Then she would once again go on another depression escapade. As if craving a different jam or brand of cereal made me ungrateful.

Freedom, to me, was silence. Not the silence of fear, but the silence of peace. I yearned for harmony. But if I spoke, confrontation would ensue. So, I learned to stay quiet. A home without tension. A life without commentary. I wrote that life down. I built it sentence by sentence.

Still, writing was a private act. No one knew about it. I had to keep my notebooks hidden. My mother would've seen it as either indulgent or suspicious—why would a boy need to write so much? What was he hiding? And so, I hid it all: my curiosity, my sensitivity, my hunger for beauty, for space, for meaning. I became good at invisibility.

Looking back, I see that my reality as a child was one of imposed identity. I was assigned a role—the good one, the easy one, the helper—and rewarded not with love, but with absence. But I was never allowed to write on my own. That was the real cage.

And so I wrote in private. That was not easy, and often an arduous endeavor. I grew up not knowing boundaries. But I needed to write not just to survive the days, but to sketch a doorway. What I didn't realize then was that writing wasn't a dream. It was a tool. And it would save me again and again.

In a house where my voice was dismissed and my choices were disregarded, my journal became the only place where I was real. I couldn't fight the rules, but I could write around them. And in doing so, I found something dangerous and exhilarating:

I had the power to imagine something else.

II. A Secret Life on Paper

I couldn't speak freely, but I could write. In a house where even birthday cake wasn't safe from override, my journal became the only place where I had complete authority. It was mine—my words, my hand, my thoughts—undiluted and uncensored. No one corrected me on those pages. No one sighed or rolled their eyes or told me I was "too sensitive" or "too much." On paper, I was allowed to exist.

Now my "record book" has become a diary, and I have learned what the word means. I found myself expressing my feelings more. I became a keen observer. Not just at home, but everywhere, school, friends' homes, neighborhood adults, people at church, stores, and store clerks. Then it hit me, why was my family so weird? I used to write about what we ate, and why we ate it. Instead of recording what I wore, I was writing why my mom made me wear this. I was fascinated by the weather. I expanded my knowledge of weather to include barometric pressure, precipitation, and the temperature at which the thermometer dropped to zero. But slowly, the entries stretched. A sentence became a paragraph. A paragraph became a reflection. Soon, I was narrating moods, observations, and the strange emotional choreography of our home—the way my mother's smile could tighten into disapproval mid-sentence, or how my father's silence after dinner felt heavier than his anger.

Mom's disapproval was evident in her eyes, which turned black as coal, and in an ominous glare. Her jaws clenched, and her lips pursed. She knew how to make herself look ugly. When upset and not getting her way or the attention she desired, she would cry to get others to offer sympathy, praise, and assurance. I loathed her behavior.

Neal's provocations, Dad's anger issues, and little brother Dean wanting to emulate his mother. That was disgusting and horrible to me.

I didn't show the notebooks to anyone. That was unthinkable. For my family to find my journal was perilous. I knew instinctively that this world I was building had to stay hidden. My mother would have been suspicious or dismissive. My father would have belittled me outright—"What are you doing, writing in a girl's diary?" he would've sneered. He saw writing as something soft, something feminine, something unbecoming of a boy. To him, introspection was weakness. And I had learned long ago that showing softness was dangerous.

But in that privacy, a different version of me began to take shape. On the page, I wasn't just the obedient son or the passive brother. I was a thinker, a dreamer, a planner. I imagined a future apartment—quiet, tidy, with my favorite foods in the fridge and books stacked just the way I liked them. I imagined long walks alone, early morning routines, and grocery shopping for myself. I imagined becoming a pharmacist—not for the science, really, but for the independence it promised. It was the job that would get me out.

I imagined clothes too—real clothes, not the polyester horrors my mother insisted on. She fancied herself as a fashion expert, but she wasn't. Her sense of style hovered somewhere between thrift store matron and Eisenhower-era modesty. As a teenager, I just wanted to look like the other boys at school. I longed for cotton shirts, wool trousers, khakis, linen blends, soft knits that didn't cling or shine. Living on my own would mean freedom from her taste. Freedom from being dressed like someone I wasn't.

More than once, I sketched maps—mental and literal—plotting how far I'd have to go to feel free. Five hundred miles became my starting line. Anything closer, and I feared I'd be pulled back in. I kept a list of cities, a calculation of distance, even considered their climates, their accents, and their potential for reinvention. Minneapolis wasn't far enough. Chicago is too familiar. But Indianapolis—it had a ring of neutrality. No one I knew had ever mentioned it. That, somehow, made it safe.

My notebooks weren't confessionals. They weren't teenage laments or dramatic screeds. They were blueprints. Quiet blueprints for a future I wasn't sure I'd ever see, but one I desperately needed to believe in. I was designing a life with more than space—I was creating a life with authorship.

There's one entry I remember exceptionally well. I must've been around 14. I wrote, "Someday I will wake up and make my toast, with cherry preserves if I want. And no one will say a word about it."

And another, written in capital letters and underlined twice: "I will buy the clothes that I like. No more polyester!"

It wasn't just about jam or fabric. It was about choice. About freedom from scrutiny. About pleasure without guilt.

Even the simple act of writing those sentences gave me power. I felt it. The way a single page could shift the weight inside me. I started to notice more clearly the lines between what I felt and what I performed. I could feel the ache of being shut out of a room I shared with my brother, and write that ache down, and suddenly, it wasn't just pain anymore. It was a story. It was true. It was a quiet defiance.

There were risks, of course. If my journals had been found, I would've had no defense. But I became clever. I switched up where I hid them. I tore out pages if they felt too revealing. I learned the art of masking intensity with detail—writing about dinner but meaning something deeper. And in this way, writing became not only therapy but training. I was learning how to observe, how to interpret, how to shape experience into meaning.

I didn't yet know I would become a writer in the formal sense. That idea felt too distant, too luxurious. But I knew this: Writing gave me back to myself. In a world that seemed determined to script my life for me, I was writing my way toward a different narrative.

And that narrative, for the first time, felt like it could be mine.

III. Crossing the 500-Mile Threshold

I did it. I got out.

It wasn't dramatic—no slammed doors or fiery speeches. Just a packed Plymouth Duster, a rented U-Haul car-top carrier, and a summer lease on a modest apartment I shared with my college friend Duane. We were both finishing our final class to graduate. The plan was simple: Finish school, leave Moorhead, and start over, far away.

I made one final stop that evening at my parents' house before leaving for Indianapolis the next day. It felt more like a duty than a goodbye. No one said much. By then, I had learned to be professional about such things—keep it calm, shake hands, and don't stir emotion. But I noticed my father was quiet, almost pensive, as if registering the weight of what was about to happen. My mother, unable to let the spotlight pass her by, began to fuss—rearranging objects on the counter, nitpicking over my packing, drawing attention. And Neal and Dean stood nearby, almost dumbfounded. Their silence said everything: *Brad is leaving us?*

And I was for good.

Crossing state lines felt like crossing into a new identity. I wasn't only driving southeast—I was moving away from invisibility, away from polyester shirts and sharing a full-sized bed, away from guilt-tripped obedience and unsolicited fashion advice. I was headed toward the life I had written about for years—one where I chose what I wore, what I ate, where I lived, and who I became.

That freedom started before I even left. During college, I had begun earning great tips as a waiter, and with the support of trusted adults, I opened a personal charge account at the Fargo Toggery—a high-end men's clothing store. It felt like stepping into another world: refined fabrics, elegant textures, real tailoring. My mother was horrified. "The Toggery? What's wrong with JCPenney's and Kmart?" she barked.

I'll never forget the outfit: a bluish-gray wool windowpane sport coat, paired with soft wool slacks, a crisp blue Oxford shirt, and a navy-blue club tie. I felt sharp, modern, and seen. But when she saw it, she gave me an earful. "That shirt is going to wrinkle; you'll have to iron it. Polyester doesn't wrinkle! And that sports coat? What a mistake. You don't know fashion like I do."

Mom knew she was losing control over me, and oh, how she despised that. I started to sound matter of fact. "Mom, that's no big deal, I drop off my dress shirts at the dry cleaners."

"Oh, you and your thinking of living on a champagne appetite on a beer income," she screeched.

"Well, Mom, I'm living on my own, paying for my room and board at the fraternity, and I'm busy with school and work. I can afford to take my clothes to the dry cleaner's. It's a matter of using my time and resources wisely," I stated, calm and confident.

Mom had one more dig. "You sure are getting full of yourself!" It was intended to be a reprimand, a chance to dish out discipline.

I calmly smiled and replied, "I've grown into a man, Mom, and there's nothing you can do about that."

I stung her with that line. Tears began to well in her eyes, not out of hurt, shame, or pain, but her self-pity and not getting what she wanted—for her boys to never grow up.

Her verdict stung, but it didn't stick. I had made sure of that. Nearly everyone else—friends, classmates, even college professors—complimented me. I walked taller in that jacket. It didn't just fit my body; it fit who I was becoming.

After graduating and moving to Indianapolis, I settled into my first apartment, modest but fully mine. I opened the refrigerator to see only what *I* had chosen to put there: eggs, milk, and cherry preserves. I toasted sourdough bread and buttered it slowly, deliberately. The kitchen buzzed with peace. No interruptions. No critiques. No commentary on my jam. Just me and my becoming.

Of course, freedom came with responsibility. There were bills to pay, meals to cook, and long hours on my feet. But even when tired, I never once wished to return to Moorhead. I was shaping a new life—900 miles away, on my terms.

Becoming a pharmacist had been the goal, and I achieved it. I passed the boards, got licensed, and had my first job. Wearing the white coat gave me a kind of pride, a signal that I was stable, professional, and respected. And I was proud. But over time, a different feeling began to creep inside that I hadn't expected.

The pharmacy had promised purpose and structure. But what it delivered was repetition, confinement, and a surprising kind of dullness. I stood for hours in the small square footage, processing prescriptions, staring at computer screens, repeating the same counsel over and over. The fluorescent lights buzzed. The energy flattened. I had escaped one cage, only to find myself in another.

One moment still makes me shake my head. A mother came in with her ten-year-old son and asked me to look at his feet. She had him take off his shoes, right there in the pharmacy. The boy winced. His toenails were yellowed, the skin cracked and raw with athlete's foot. She leaned in and asked, "What do you recommend?"

I gave her options: Lamisil, tolnaftate, and miconazole. I explained that fungal infections are slow to heal, and treatment takes time and consistency. She frowned at the prices. She frowned harder at the timeline. I kept calm, trying to educate. Then she said, "Forget it. I'm just going to put kerosene on his feet. That'll fix it."

And with that, she grabbed her son's hand, and they sped off. I stood behind the counter, dumbfounded.

That moment didn't break me, but it added another layer to my disillusionment. I was trained, licensed, and trying to help people, and sometimes they just wanted quick fixes or folk remedies. I began to wonder if this was it. Was this the life I had dreamed of being?

I hated conflict, and I still do. I seek harmony. The opioid addiction took its toll on me and was the central tipping point for wanting out of retail pharmacy. In many instances, we would triple-count 60 tablets of Vicodin. A tech and I made sure we dispensed exactly 60, like the prescription said. One early afternoon, a patient came in angry. "You shorted me on my Vicodin." I assured him we dispensed 60, and we triple-count to ensure accuracy.

"Did you hear me?" he screamed. "I said you shorted me 20 tablets!" "That can't be, sir. We triple-count our controlled drug prescriptions." Then he erupted. "Are you calling me a goddamn liar?" He was agitated. I said, "No, perhaps you misplaced some." It was now getting ugly, and he was drawing attention in the store, exactly what he wanted to do.

"Are you going to give me more tablets or not?" he demanded. I said, "No, I'm not. Our staff has confirmed our count of 60 tablets." He fumed out of the store. "I'm calling your home office."

Sure enough, he did. The non-pharmacist manager reprimanded me severely. I was written up for bad customer service and relations. The chain gave him a $50 gift certificate. I had to give him 20 more tablets, and lastly, I had to write him a letter of apology.

I was making my strategy to get out of retail pharmacy!

Still, the core of my freedom remained. I had escaped the orbit of my mother. I had chosen a life where I picked my shirts, my meals, my morning routines. I remembered the boy who had once written, "No more polyester." That boy had been right. Freedom wasn't loud. It was cotton. It was toast with preserves. It was an apartment with quiet air. It was the space to wonder who I was.

I had crossed the 500-mile threshold. But the real distance between the life I was living and the life I longed to write was only beginning to reveal itself.

IV. Returning to the Page—This Time for Real

There comes a point when you realize freedom isn't just about leaving somewhere. It's about arriving somewhere truer within yourself.

I had left Moorhead. I had become a pharmacist. I had my own space, my income, and a closet full of soft cotton shirts, khakis, and wool slacks that *I* had chosen. By most measures, I had succeeded. But something inside me began to ache again—not with urgency, but with a kind of dull hum, like a song I couldn't quite hear but couldn't tune out either.

The pharmacy counter had its structure, its rhythm. But it lacked resonance. I was doing good work, but it wasn't nourishing me. I missed thinking deeply, observing the world, interpreting it—not through dosage labels and drug interactions, but through story, insight, and reflection.

And so, quietly, I returned to the page.

It didn't start with a declaration. I didn't sit down and say, "I'm a writer now." I just began to write again. Not the old lists and blueprints of escape, but memories. Fragments. Moments that had stayed with me. I wrote about Dean and me sharing that small bed, about the lemon cake I never got, about the wool sport coat that made me feel alive in a room where I wasn't supposed to shine.

What surprised me was how much was still there—buried, unprocessed, waiting. The stories hadn't disappeared. They had been patient. And now, they came back with texture, emotion, and clarity I hadn't expected. My younger self, so often silenced, finally had something to say.

Writing was no longer just an act of escape. It became an act of *reclamation*.

I wrote about my mother, not with revenge, but with revelation. I traced her need for control, her envy, her rules, her need to define everything in black and white. I no longer needed to argue with her or win her over. On the page, I simply told the truth. That was enough. Writing her with honesty, not bitterness, gave me power. It gave me peace.

I wrote about my father, not just his anger, but the fear underneath it. I began to see him not just as an enforcer of Mom's moods, but as a man in over his head, afraid of being small, fearful of losing control. I didn't absolve him. But I understood him more clearly when I wrote him down.

I wrote about Neal. About Dean. About the role I played in our family—"too good for your good," as my father once said. I examined what that phrase had done to me—how it trained me to self-abandon, to anticipate everyone's needs but my own, to mistake invisibility for virtue. And I wrote about the cost of that kind of goodness: the aching need for validation, the endless hunger to be seen, the fear of making anyone uncomfortable—even on the page.

Piece by piece, I began to reclaim my own story—not the one I had to live, but the one I chose to tell.

The page didn't judge. It didn't interrupt. It didn't compare me to anyone else. And in writing, I didn't just rediscover my voice—I started to forgive it. To trust it. To believe it had something worthwhile to say.

Eventually, writing became more than journaling. I began crafting essays. I wrote about leadership, about human behavior, about observation, reflection, and resilience. I found my way into grant writing—a strange, beautiful intersection of storytelling and advocacy. I wrote to lift others, to help organizations thrive, to make a case for something better. And that, too, became a form of healing.

One unexpected turning point came during my time in biomedical sales. I wasn't aiming to become "a writer." But I helped a professor revise and strengthen a grant proposal—

and he won. Word got around. Academia took notice. Colleagues began to seek me out not just for products or services, but for my way with words. In those circles, I quietly became known not as the former pharmacist or salesman but as the *writer.*

Still, some stories took more courage than others.

The essay I'm most proud of, "Held to the Shore," was one I was afraid to write. It reached into vulnerable territory, both emotionally and personally. I almost didn't do it. But I pressed forward. And once it was on the page, I knew: This was the story I'd been carrying for decades. I've since sent it to several literary reviews in different forms. Each time, it feels like sending a part of myself out into the world—fragile but free.

The boy who once scribbled quietly under a blanket, afraid of being caught with a pen in hand, had become a man whose words made an impact, opened doors, and built bridges.

And still, writing kept me honest. It reminded me that no life is ever entirely escaped, only better understood. The ghosts of control, guilt, and performance still show up from time to time. But now, I meet them with a pen.

Writing, once a secret, has become my compass. Not to run away—but to return. To myself. To the truth. To others.

V. A New Reality—and a New Voice

There's a moment in life when you realize: You're no longer dreaming the future—you're living the one you wrote.

It didn't happen all at once. There was no trumpet blast announcing my transformation. But slowly, quietly, sentence by sentence, I became someone I trust. Someone I like. Someone who no longer seeks permission to exist.

That's what writing has done for me.

It began as a way to survive—to sketch a world where I had freedom, privacy, and voice. Then it became a way to escape—Moorhead, my mother's grasp, the scripts that were never mine. Then it became something more potent than either survival or escape: it became *clarity*.

Writing gave me the ability to see my life not just as a string of events, but as a narrative. One I could shape, revisit, and revise. I could name what had once been confusing. I could speak what had once been forbidden. And in doing so, I gave others the courage to do the same.

I still hear my mother's voice sometimes when I try something bold. I still feel the old twinge of guilt when I succeed. But I meet those echoes with awareness now—with compassion, even. They don't define me anymore. They remind me of how far I've come.

I still write about the past—but now with purpose. I write to help others name their silences. To recognize the cages they were born into. To remind them that the act of writing—of *truthfully narrating* your own life—is a form of freedom no one can take away.

Through essays, memoirs, grants, blogs, and even my newsletter, I connect with others who are also searching for meaning, for authenticity, for breath. And what I've learned is this: You don't have to be a professional writer to write a new reality.

You just have to be honest.

You just have to start.

Sometimes, people ask me if I wish I had taken a different path earlier, changed careers sooner, gone back to school, or written books in my thirties. But I've stopped measuring my life by *when*.

I measure it now by *how fully* I live it.

And how fully I tell it.

That's what writing has taught me. And that is the gift I now offer others—through stories, essays, mentorship, encouragement, and witness.

There is no one moment when we are saved.

But there are moments when we realize:

We are no longer lost.

Writing didn't just help me survive one life.

It taught me how to write the one I needed.

And in doing so, I discovered the truth that saved me:

We are not born into the stories we must live.

We are born with the power to write our way out.

And to the boy who once dreamed of cherry preserves and cotton shirts, I would say this:

Don't stop writing, even when it feels pointless. Don't stop dreaming, even when they roll their eyes. The toast, the jam, the shirt—they're not just things. They're symbols of something far bigger: choice, freedom, dignity. You won't just wear what you want. You'll become who you are. And you'll do it with grace.

My New Non-Human Body

Joanne Gram

Grandmother said get over yourself

You have all it takes to become yourself

    whatever yourself needs

And so I do

I can make it work
Think myself into a range of colors
    an arrangement of keen eyes and ears
        gotta touch and understand
           what the touchings mean

Today I may have green hair
    speckled feathers around my
        nether regions   a mouth for tasting
    wide-waisted like a well-basted turkey
        on some holiday we can rename after dinner

Not taking the form of predator or prey
    Stay neutral and only consume
        the seasonings of essences around me
            become the best parts of what I eat
                to stay seated at the infinite
                    banquet table of life and
                    death

When creatures appear to measure me
    for profit or loss   I can gloss away
        like a slick cosmetic lotion   slide
            off into an ocean of undulating
                words   phrases
                eliciting random praises

I can reshape into my gossamer oblivion
    to reappear in unrelenting fashion
        assume my chosen amber throne
            on my own amorphous pavilion
                my own resilient passion to
                survive

And so I do

Mango Tree

Nuriya Mirakbar

Weaving with golden thread
every seam of me comes undone
unraveling my soul to become new.

I dream of a white house with a mango tree
and the fruit there knows no winter
my baby smells of spring.

One must let go to hold another
so like a careless child I slowly start
to let go of the colorful balloons.

I dream of becoming a bird
the sky shall know me by name
the clouds and the stars, they kiss me.

My leaves remember blossoming
as the wind begins to carry them away
to a new land with a different sun.

I dream of a life full with vivid sunsets
and there my mother cradles my baby on the porch
the crickets sing to us all night long.

Let me go so I can go to the mango tree
and let me step into the binds of eternity
because there I shall peacefully sleep.

Whole: A Meditation in Prose
Betsy McDaniel Boyer

You are ready.
Dressed for the party, with an inner glow of eagerness.
  The doors before you stand ready,
      there is excitement, anticipation,
      but no anxiety.
      hand on knob, ready to turn.

Step inside, there is a spotlight on you,
      warm, welcoming
      like immersion in water at the perfect
      temperature.
Applause surrounds, a pleasant roar,
      your eyes adjust and begin to see figures
      before you; they form an aisle.
Smiles greet you,
      at times some tears.
      as you recognize them.

Each face was you,
      as toddler, teenager, versions of adulthood.
Each overjoyed that you have finally arrived
      here, ready to remember.
One by one they approach, opening their arms,
      you take each embrace, feeling who you were.
You cradle a newborn baby you,
      new to the planet.

Each time your arms encircle a version of you,
   gratitude deepens as each moment of your
  existence is absorbed,
 and your light grows brighter.

Slight movement is there, in the shadows,
   just outside your growing light.
One by one, figures appear, some mere outlines
 some devoid of color, monochrome.
They are moments hidden away
   versions cast into darkness, left behind
 for the sake of survival and forward motion.

They carry experiences of heartbreak and shame,
   your guilt and your rage.
You hold no fear and allow the emotion they carry
   to manifest between you.
 you see it as a solid entity, separate.
The edges glint like steel, and you remember
 feeling those cuts,
 remember the bleeding.

Then, stepping forward, opening your arms,
   they, tentatively, open theirs.
The embrace ignites each memory,
   flame clears that old sentiment that tried to
   stay solid,
   leaving only a wisp of smoke fading into the
   air.
The cause of that pain is erased, leaving
   recognition of what that version of you
 had to endure,
   the lesson learned
   and only grace remains.

You turn and are suddenly alone.
In a place you love deeply.
Shining your bright light so wide,
   you cannot see the edges.
And here you begin
   again
 here you stand in authenticity.

   Whole.
   Ready for the next step,
      the next inhale,
      the next embrace.